TWO LOVES

Bill is handsome, tender and exciting, but Cherry knows she can't live on love alone. Phillip doesn't attract her like Bill does, but his wealth can buy her everything she's always wanted. Cherry is determined to have them both. Cleverly concealing one's existence from the other, she begins leading a dangerous double life, unknowingly pushing all three of them towards disaster . . .

DENISE ROBINS

◆

TWO LOVES

Complete and Unabridged

LINFORD
Leicester

First published in Great Britain in 1954

First Linford Edition
published 2018

A catalogue record for this book is available
from the British Library.

ISBN 978–1–4448–3940–1

Published by
F. A. Thorpe (Publishing)
Anstey, Leicestershire

Set by Words & Graphics Ltd.
Anstey, Leicestershire
Printed and bound in Great Britain by
T. J. International Ltd., Padstow, Cornwall

This book is printed on acid-free paper

1

Even as a child Cherry Brown had longed for money and the things money could buy and wanted to be the centre of attraction wherever she went.

Her mother had often told her that when she was a tiny tot of four or five, she would preen herself in front of a mirror, satisfy herself that she looked 'nice,' then run out and join her small playmates in the village; expect to be the leading spirit of the games and the queen of all the small boys. She was 'Queen of the May' every summer, and she was belle of the village from her 'teens. She loved to feel that she was fascinating, that she had a strong appeal and charm for everybody, and while she accepted the simple, humble devotion of the country lads, she really disdained it; told herself that she would be a fool not to use her beauty and charm to climb the social ladder.

Yes, looking back now, she realised it was a sort of craze in her to be rich and adored. It burned inside her like a flame, although she had to live her life for a time where Fate had placed her — in Dalescombe as a domestic servant to the local doctor.

Cherry longed for love; but she wasn't going to throw herself away on some farm boy or garage-hand. Her head ruled her heart. Her lover must be rich. And so, until she was eighteen, she kept herself away from the Dalescombe boys.

She cut out photographs of the glamour girls and models from old Society papers which some lady in the village had finished with, and plastered the walls of her tiny attic-bedroom at home with them. Titled women of fashion and film stars were her models. She intended to look like they looked. One day she intended to wear smart clothes with a good deal more grace than they wore them! She even bought an old book of etiquette from a second-hand bookshop and studied it.

Then love came into Cherry's life. Not money, not any of the luxuries for which her soul yearned; but passionate love, as thrilling, as wonderful as any girl could desire. They are fools who say that there is no love at first sight.

There was a fair at Dalescombe every June. This particular June there was to be a small boxing contest. The local light, Ted Stevens, was to box a boy named Bill Carew from Little Cross, a village about ten miles away.

Cherry's brother, Eric, took her along to the fair. He wanted to see the boxing match, and that is how she first met Bill Carew. He was then twenty-two, and only a motor mechanic at Little Cross, but he had more brains, more culture, and more charm than most of her friends. She was hard to please, but when she set her eyes on Bill when he came into the ring, she thought him the handsomest chap she'd ever seen.

Tall, of middle weight, he had magnificent shoulders, the long reach, the iron hands of a born boxer. The muscles rippled beautifully under his smooth, bronzed skin, and he had a fine head covered with dark, curly hair, a pair of amazingly blue eyes — his mother was Irish — and a rich beguiling voice. Cherry fell in love with those handsome, Irish eyes with their black lashes and his caressing voice just as soon as she met him.

One of the girls from Little Cross who knew her sister — who was a telephonist, told her that Bill Carew had no girlfriends.

'Everyone says he's hard to please,' she informed Cherry. 'Smiles at all the girls and no more. Plenty have tried to catch him but he seems hard to get.'

That was a challenge, and Cherry's heart thrilled in response.

Cherry knew she was looking pretty that night in her pink dress, with best best nylons covering slim legs — one of her good points; her hair, which was bright chestnut brown, in disorder about her face. She had pink cheeks and lustrous, hazel eyes, and attractive curved lips. She meant to make that young chap, who was so handsome and so 'particular,' take notice of her.

Cherry said to her sister's friend:

'I bet you I'll catch him, Polly!'

Bill Carew had at that moment moved away from a circle of small boy admirers after the fight. He was just getting astride one of the rocking-horses on the merry-go-round. The music was playing noisily. Bright lights flared. All the boys and girls were laughing and shouting. It was a warm June night, alive with gaiety, with simple pleasures that satisfied Cherry's ambitious soul for once. She had eyes only for the handsome young boxer on his horse.

The whistle shrilled. The horses began to move round, and her heart was pounding, her eyes riveted on Bill. The next instant she sprang onto the merry-go-round and clutched his arm.

5

'I'm going on your horse with you!' Cherry said, panting,

He smiled quickly and stared at her in amazement. She smiled, and, as light as thistle-down, jumped on to the horse in front of him.

'Catch hold, Bill Carew!' she said daringly.

Polly and her sister, open-mouthed, awed at her daring stood watching on the green. And then, a new, eager look came into Bill Carew's blue eyes. He put an arm about her.

'You've got nerve, you little thing. But all right, hold on. I've got you!'

Round went the horses, swaying, rocking to the music. The lights, the faces on the green became a kaleidoscope of colour. She looked up into the eyes of the man who held her close to him and laughed.

'You boxed beautifully,' she whispered. 'I'm glad you laid Ted out.'

'Thanks!' he said. 'That's nice of you. What's your name?'

'Cherry Brown,' she told him.

'Cherry's a pretty name,' he said, and stared down at her. She saw him taking in her looks, saw him becoming very aware of the pink of her cheeks and the length of her lashes and her smile. Before that merry-go-round stopped Bill Carew was holding her just a little tighter.

When it slowed down, Cherry jumped out of his arms and on to the ground.

'Good-night!' she said archly.

But he was after her like a shot.

'Don't run away. Come and have a dance,' he begged.

She danced with him quite demurely; saw he was puzzled by her; didn't know what to make of her. She was shy and bold in turns. She interested him. Finally, he led her across the clover fields, to the fringe of Dalescombe Woods. And there, suddenly, took her in his arms and kissed her.

Cherry's feelings were indescribable when she felt that kiss on her lips. She had flirted before, kissed lightly, but

7

never had love touched her as it did with Bill's first kiss. She wanted nothing, nobody but Bill Carew from Little Cross that night — Bill with his curly black hair and Irish blue eyes and warm and bronzed young face.

'Cherry, Cherry, how wonderful you are, you little thing. Sure, I felt something strange and wonderful happening to me when you jumped up on the merry-go-round with me. You were so cheeky and adorable.'

She looked at him. Her desire for riches was completely in the background then. She said:

'I love you, Bill! You're so strong, darling! I love you!'

'Say you'll walk out with me whenever I can cycle over from Little Cross to see you,' he begged. 'Say you'll marry me one day, Cherry.'

'Marriage!' Ah, that made Cherry hide her face on his breast and bite her lips. She was afraid of marriage where there was no money. Bill was telling her about himself. He cherished hopes of finding a backer to finance him; train him to become a middle-weight champion. At the moment in Little Cross he was a hero, but in the world — nothing. And his ambitions like hers, might come to nothing.

Cherry knew she could not marry on bread and cheese and kisses. But that night of the fair she was reckless — stupid with love. When she walked back to the fair with him to find her brother, she had promised to marry Bill Carew.

It was a great victory, and Cherry loved Bill Carew that night, and for many days after. But could she marry him? He wasn't able to buy her the flowers and jewels and furs like the lover of her dreams. She was determined to be a rich man's wife.

Suddenly she remembered that some new people had taken the Manor House, Dalescombe — a beautiful old Georgian residence, which stood in sixty acres of grounds. They wanted a parlour-maid. Most of Cherry's girlfriends refused to go into domestic jobs. But she thought a living-in post in a luxurious home might be amusing. And one was well paid on the staff there. Besides, she would catch glimpses of life — real life! She would be able to see how ladies lived in their own houses — rich ladies, what they said, how they behaved. She could take note: model herself on them. She would listen and learn.

Cherry wrote to Lady Bayfield, who had taken the Manor House, and asked if she would give her a trial. To her delight she was accepted.

Cherry told Bill about the new job one night when he cycled over from Little Cross to meet her at their trysting-place down by the woods. But the thrill of the new situation had gone. She had Bill's arms about her then, his lips on hers. She wanted nothing but him. Her restless heart was at peace.

'If only I was rich and could marry you,' he said in a yearning voice, his blue eyes shining down at her in the starlight. 'Cherry, little girl, I do love you!'

'I adore you!' she answered. 'I wish we could marry now.'

He jumped off the stile on which they had been sitting, like any Dalescombe sweethearts, and circled her waist with his arms. His face had grown suddenly hard and white.

'Cherry, you lovely little thing, if ever you throw me over — I'll want to kill you!'

Her heart gave a leap of fear. She put her hands on his head.

'Bill darling, I don't want to throw you over.'

'But if you ever do. You're so pretty, so fascinating. I'm terribly afraid some fellow will try and steal you, and if he did I'd put a bullet in his head!'

Then on the eighteenth of that sweet mad month of June, Cherry entered Lady Bayfield's service — her first place 'sleeping-in' — and the whole course of her life altered from that day onward.

Lady Bayfield was a widow. She had a large income, an old aristocratic title, and one daughter, her heiress, by name Veronica.

Veronica was, in her way, a very pretty girl. She was one year older than Cherry, and a woman of the world.

She had had all the chances that life had not given to Cherry — expensive education and an adoring mother to give her everything, within reason, that she wanted.

Cherry used to wonder how her charm would stand against Veronica's. By some strange whim of Fate's Cherry was given the chance a month after she became one of the staff at the Manor House.

Veronica went away for three weeks to stay with an aunt in London. When she came back she brought a fiancé for her mother's approval. Lady Bayfield approved. The young man — Phillip Bellairs — was not titled, but he had an extremely rich father — one of the big shipbuilders of England — who indulged his whims, and one day he would inherit a fortune.

He had been educated at Eton and Oxford. He was about twenty-seven years old, had travelled a good deal, was very intelligent, and considered an excellent 'catch'. He had a shooting lodge in Scotland, lived either with his parents in their London house, or at his exclusive club, and owned racehorses at Newmarket.

Hearing all this, Cherry began to envy Veronica. She had all Cherry wanted. Phillip Bellairs seemed to be just the man of her desires.

She caught a glimpse of him in the hall just before dinner. He was slim, shorter than Bill Carew by a head, but very good-looking. He had smooth, brown hair, brushed straight off his forehead. His face was thin and a little lined for his age.

In no way was Phillip Bellairs as handsome or as arresting as Bill Carew. But much more fascinating to Cherry from that night onwards! He had so much more than good looks. He had money, and money was power.

Cherry watched him closely for several days and nights. She saw Veronica had attracted him. Her ash-blonde hair, her sweet manner, her flattery of him. He was weak, and weak men succumb so easily to flattery.

When Cherry helped her dress one night for a dinner-party celebrating their engagement down at the Manor House, she asked Cherry if she thought she 'looked nice'.

'Lovely, Miss!' Cherry answered. But to herself she said 'Humph! Who wouldn't look nice in a Dior Model costing £100 or more. I'd look a good deal prettier than you, my lady, Veronica, in that frock.' She knew because she had tried it on one night.

Cherry had made up her mind then and there to win the attention of Phillip Bellairs — to use her charm against Veronica's. She wanted to be rich and vowed to satisfy her ambition through Phillip Bellairs.

She forgot Bill. She was away from the loving thrall in which he held her when she was in his arms. She had not seen him for several days.

Cherry waited at table that night, helping old Masters, the butler. The dining-room was full of dim light from the tall wax candles on the rich mahogany table. It looked very handsome with its flowers and Georgian silver and glittering glass.

Cherry caught Phillip Bellairs' eye once, then he looked away again quite indifferently. She thought, with anger in her heart:

'Not going to take notice of me — eh? Your sort don't look at staff, except as machines — eh? You wait!'

She leaned over his right shoulder to pick up his empty hock glass. She was clearing the table for dessert. Masters held the silver tray behind her. Deliberately her fingers clenched on the glass — clenched until it smashed to fragments in her hand. She dropped the pieces and gave a little cry.

'Oh dear!'

The blood spurted from one or two cuts on Cherry's finger. The colour left her cheeks, not so much with the pain as the excitement of that moment. She had achieved her ambition! Phillip Bellairs sprang to his feet and took decided notice of her.

'Please let me help you,' he drawled courteously.

'I-I'm so dreadfully sorry, your ladyship,' Cherry said in a trembling voice to Lady Bayfield.

'So unlike you to have accidents, Cherry,' she replied, graciously enough.

But Veronica's eyes regarded her sullenly. Despite Cherry's protests, Phillip had whipped a white silk handkerchief from his pocket and wound it round her cut hand.

'Oh, thank you, sir!' she said, under her breath.

Cherry looked up at him. His fingers just touched hers. And then she broke into the smile that she had practised so often. He flushed and looked away very quickly. But during the rest of dinner his eyes, from time to time, roved to her face with a half-nervous, half-eager look. She existed for Phillip Bellairs now, not as a servant, but as a pretty, attractive girl.

Next morning Cherry was dusting the drawing-room before the family was down. Mr. Phillip Bellairs strolled into the room through the French windows from the sunlit garden. It was a gorgeous summer morning, and he had taken an early stroll.

'Ah, good-morning!' he said. 'How's the cut hand?'

'It was nothing, thank you!' Cherry said. 'The cuts weren't deep. It was kind of you to lend me this.'

She took his ironed handkerchief out of her apron pocket and handed it to him.

'So beautifully washed,' he murmured. 'Thank you — er — what's your name?'

'Cherry Brown.'

He said: 'I love eating cherries!'

She laughed. He amused her. Cherry suddenly knelt down at his feet to wipe up some ash that had fallen on the parquet floor from his cigarette.

'Oh, how thoughtless of me! I'll do it, Cherry,' he said.

He stooped. Deliberately she looked up. She could see that his eyes were greenish hazel, rather lazy, indolent. He suddenly flushed.

'You're a sight too pretty to be let loose in this world, Cherry,' he said.

But Cherry wasn't going to let him imagine he could just snatch a kiss and then run away. She was too clever for that. She had more sense than Veronica with her gushing and clinging.

'If you'll pardon me, I think you're much too bold,' she said, and ran out of the room. She knew she left him amazed and intrigued. He had imagined her easy to conquer. He was used to women falling in love with him. He was spoiled, overflattered by Veronica. And Cherry had, so to speak, snapped her fingers in his face and run away.

Phillip Bellairs, although so newly engaged, thought about Cherry a good many times that day.

He returned to London to his family the next morning, and Cherry didn't see him again for three weeks.

When he came down to the Manor House again it was in August. He was to stay for a fortnight with the Bayfields. Cherry noticed at once that his interest in Veronica was waning. But she knew that he had not forgotten her. She was in the hall as he passed through on his way upstairs. Masters had gone ahead with the luggage. Veronica was talking to her mother in the loggia.

He stopped in front of Cherry and gave her a funny look.

'Well, Cherry-ripe, I must say you're looking even prettier than ever, and I may as well tell you I'm feeling much bolder!' he said.

Cherry laughed and gave him a sweeping glance from under her long, curving lashes.

'Well, sir, I fancy there's a saying about 'faint heart not winning fair lady',' she said impudently.

'You darling!' he said under his breath, then had to pass on, as Veronica came running up with 'Are you all right? Do you want a drink, Phillip?'

Cherry watched him as he looked at her. Oh, yes, he was bored with her by now! She had 'gushed' all the love out of him. He was no longer in love with her. But he was just a little bit keen about Cherry, and she did everything in her power to fan the flame she'd lit. She thought little about Bill these days, and much about Phillip Bellairs and his money. Yet only the night before she had met Bill. He had come in from Little Cross to tell her of his latest triumph — how he had boxed with a fellow from Whitechapel, and knocked him out in three rounds.

She felt restless in his arms that night. She loved him. What was Phillip compared to this man? A weakling. Bill could knock him down with one blow.

Oh, and the Irish eyes of her lover and that beguiling voice!

'Cherry, dearest, put your lips on mine and tell me you love me still,' he whispered, with his great arms straining her to him.

And then she found it hard to resist. She did not want anything but those kisses of Bill's. She left him hating herself for the deliberate way in which she meant to try to attract Veronica's fiancé.

It was like a thrilling, dangerous game — playing with fire, secretly pitting her strength against Veronica Bayfield's. She did not know it. She only knew that her fair, babyish beauty and her charm were losing their attraction for her fiancé. Cherry saw it. When she was in the room, serving the meals at dinner-time, bringing in afternoon tea with Masters, wherever it was, Phillip Bellairs' restless eyes followed her figure and tried to meet her gaze. Cherry avoided that gaze until just before she left the room, then gave him a challenging little look which made him bite his lip and search restlessly in his pockets for cigarettes and lighter.

2

One afternoon Cherry was shaking up the sofa cushions in the drawing-room and tidying books and papers. Lady Bayfield was resting at this hour. Veronica had gone up to town for the day to see her dentist. She had been suffering from toothache.

Phillip Bellairs strolled into the drawing-room just as she was preparing to leave it. It was one of those hot, drowsy days in late August. The sun-blinds were drawn and the big drawing-room, a study in pale green and mauve, looked cool and inviting. He barred her exit from the room, leaning against the closed doors, hands thrust deep in his pockets. He gave her a long, strange look from his narrow eyes.

'Well, you little devil,' he said. 'And how are you?'

'I am well, thank you, sir,' Cherry said coolly.

'You look as radiant as a summer rose,' he said.

'Pardon me, I haven't time for listening to compliments, sir,' she said.

'You must make time if I want to pay you compliments!' he said angrily. 'I won't have you being so cool and proud with me, you little witch!'

Cherry tried to brush past him. Of course, he took her arm. She knew he would.

'Please let me go!' she said.

'Kiss me first!' he said in a low voice.

'Certainly not! How dare you!' she said, stifling a laugh.

He took her other arm and forced her to face him.

'I've been watching you for days,' he said, breathing very fast. 'And you've been challenging me, maddening me. Yes, you can't deny it. Looking so exquisite with your bright pink cheeks and hazel eyes. Cherry, kiss me — quickly.'

'I won't!' she said. 'You're engaged to Veronica and you ought to be ashamed.'

'Dam' it, I don't care!' Phillip Bellairs was losing control of himself. All the weakness in his character was uppermost, and Cherry did her best to fan the flames she had lit in him by just opposing his wishes.

'Let me go!' she said, struggling.

Phillip Bellairs' husky voice said against her ear:

'Cherry, you little darling, there's something about you to drive a man crazy. Won't you kiss me?'

'I wouldn't dream of kissing a man I wasn't engaged to!' she said.

He regarded her with an exasperated look in his eyes.

'Are you engaged, Cherry-ripe?'

'Yes, thank you!'

'Who is the fellow? You let him kiss you — eh?'

'Of course!' — passionately. Her voice trembled into laughter. It amused her to exasperate Phillip Bellairs. She saw his eye darken with passion. He caught her in his arms.

'Look, I won't stand it! If some boorish farmhand is allowed to kiss you, why shouldn't I? I will — I must! Cherry — '

'You are much too bold,' she said, wriggling right out of his grasp. 'And I will not kiss any man but the man I marry!'

Cherry ran out of the drawing-room, leaving him there thwarted, his eyes more tormented than ever.

That night poor Veronica returned from her dentist, looking very pale and plain. She demanded much sympathy from Phillip Bellairs. He gave it courteously, but his eyes scarcely left Cherry's face. She went to bed quivering with excitement. Just how much did this man want her by now? Just how far would he be prepared to go for the sake of her kisses, she wondered?

Every morning Cherry had letters from Bill Carew — letters that breathed passionate love and belief in her. He was going up to Coventry for his garage to fetch down a new car; would not see her for some days. Even in the midst of her thrilling game with Phillip she wanted Bill. She was haunted by the memory of his wonderful Irish eyes, his rich voice, the touch of his strong hands, the thrill of his lips against hers. She loved Bill. She cried all night one night after she had read his letters through from beginning to end, reproached herself, wished she were more worthy of the love of a man like Bill Carew. But the moment she came in contact with Phillip Bellairs again, and remembered the power of the fortune behind him, she forgot her remorse. Her bitter feelings were submerged once again in the desire for all that money could buy.

Cherry had two more scenes with Phillip Bellairs before his stay at the Manor House came to a close. The last took place one night when the summer moonlight was flooding the grounds of the Manor. She was strolling through the orchard alone after work was over, a little green coat concealing her white overall.

Phillip came striding down the path, an attractive enough figure in his smart evening-clothes.

He greeted her with a half-longing, half-angry look.

'Well, Cherry, still cold and disdainful?'

'Neither,' she answered, giving him a significant look. 'But I'm not the sort of girl to want a man's kisses without much more.'

'What more do you want?'

'What you cannot give,' she answered, her heart pounding in her breast. 'You belong to Veronica Bayfield.'

He said, 'She isn't as attractive as you, Cherry. I've come to the end of my tether! I'm at absolute breaking point.'

'Oh!' she said, watching him under her lashes.

'I am, and you know it. I shall break

my engagement with Veronica Bayfield to-morrow!'

'Will you?' Cherry drew a little nearer him.

'Yes; I'm sick of her — sick to death!' he said hoarsely.

'Aren't you sick of me?' she teased.

'You haven't given me much chance. I'm mad for the touch of your lips, Cherry. Kiss me! Oh, darling, kiss me!'

'Oh, wait, please!' she said shakily. 'You forget I'm engaged.'

'You're going to promise yourself to me.'

'D'you want me so much?'

'Too much, Cherry!'

He was white and shaking. Cherry looked beautiful in the moonlight. He put a hand on her silky brown hair.

'Lovely — exquisite!' he muttered.

She shivered as he caught one of her arms between his fingers. She did not love this man. She loved Bill. Yet she wanted Phillip's money more than Bill's love.

'Phillip,' she whispered.

The sound of his Christian name on her lips seemed to madden him. He swung her wholly into his arms.

'Cherry, let me kiss you!'

'No. I've told you I won't kiss any but the man I'm going to marry!'

'Will you marry me, then?' Phillip asked.

'You mean that?' Her heart leaped and shook in her breast. Here was victory and a complete one. Veronica, with her lovely clothes and her titled mother had lost. Poor insignificant Cherry had won.

'I mean it, yes!' he said. His voice was reluctant. But he wanted her so much he was willing to promise anything. He even slipped off his signet-ring and put it on her finger. 'Take that if you don't believe me,' he whispered. 'I'll marry you at once, but it must be kept quiet.'

'Why?' Cherry was at once suspicious.

'Because I depend on my father for all my cash. He wants me to marry well. He'd cut me out if he knew I married you. But if I break with Veronica and just go abroad my father won't say anything. He gives me as much as I want. Later — he isn't very strong — I'll be my own master. Then I'll acknowledge you.'

'You swear that?'

'I do, Cherry. You're lovely enough to grace any man's table,' he said, his eyes glittering at her. 'And you're adorably maddening. You don't bore me as Veronica does.'

Cherry gave a low laugh.

'You'll like having me for a wife, Phillip?'

'Yes,' he said. 'We'll get married by special licence in London this very next week and go straight over to Paris. I mean it, Cherry, and you shall have everything money can buy!'

Her head whirled.

'Will you?' he asked her. 'Cherry, say you will!'

'Very well,' she said, her cheeks hot, her eyes brilliant. 'You make the

31

arrangements and book the seats to Paris.'

'Listen!' he said, seizing her hands. 'We must be careful. This must not get to my father's ears. I shall tell the Bayfields I've got important business in town, and go off first thing in the morning. I won't rouse suspicion by breaking the engagement till I've gone. Then I can write to Veronica. And you, Cherry — '

'Lady Bayfield is always kind,' she said. 'She'll give me a few days' holiday. I'll tell my mother I'm going to an aunt who lives in Brighton. I used to stay with her sometimes when I was a child.'

'And instead you'll join me in town. Oh, Cherry!' he said longingly.

'Good-night, Phillip,' she whispered.

The next morning Phillip told the Bayfields he had received an urgent message calling him to London, and departed in his car. He did not see Cherry alone — no opportunity presented itself — but he gave her a long, ardent look which told her that he was as unchanged as ever in his desire for her and they had arranged that he would send her an express letter with all instructions to her cottage home.

That evening. Cherry received a note from Bill. She felt sick and worried when she read it. It asked her to meet him down by the woods after dinner that night. He wanted to see her urgently.

She met him, and the moment she saw his face — it looked hard and fierce, yet wonderfully handsome in the starlight — she knew that something was wrong.

'What's up, Bill?' she asked.

'Cherry,' he whispered, 'I love you better than life itself, but I'm jealous of you. I've told you before I'd kill any chap who took you from me, didn't I?'

'Darling, what on earth . . . '

'Listen!' he said. 'I saw a chap at Little Cross yesterday who knows the chauffeur that works for Mr. Bellairs who's engaged to Miss Bayfield.'

'Well?' she asked.

33

'There's a rumour,' said Bill, 'that he's interested in you. Is it true?'

Cherry did not know what to reply.

She realised then and there that she wanted both these men — needed them both — Bill because she loved him, Phillip for his money. She was determined not to lose either of them.

Bill took her into his great arms and looked straight into her eyes.

'Cherry, Cherry,' he said passionately, 'swear it isn't true about this chap or I'll knock him into a jelly, and I'll — I'll choke the life out of you! Oh!' He broke off suddenly, fell at her feet on the dew-wet grass. 'Oh, my darling, my dear, I love you so — you drive me crazy!' he added brokenly. 'Say you're true to me! Put me out of my agony, Cherry!'

She would have guaranteed that there wasn't a girl on earth who could have resisted her Bill when he spoke like that — when he made a thrilling desperate appeal for love and loyalty. Cherry, who loved him, certainly could not resist

— did not wish to. The thought of Phillip and her forthcoming marriage to him faded from her mind. Some folk might say she was foolish, promising to marry one man and cherishing such a love for another at the same time. But it is possible, and only too often done. Phillip Bellairs she wanted for his money and position. Bill Carew she wanted because he was the love of her life. She just put her arms around him and covered his curly head with kisses.

'I love you — I'll be true to you. Darling, don't be afraid!' she said.

'You mean it, Cherry,' he whispered. 'You swear that there's no foundation in what the chauffeur said about you and young Bellairs?'

Cherry's heart pounded. The blood rushed to her cheeks. She was ashamed of herself and the lie she had to tell. But she told it.

'No foundation at all,' she answered him. 'Fancy you thinking for a second such a thing! I can't say it's very nice of you.'

Bill stood up. He dashed the perspiration from his forehead with the back of his hand, shut his eyes a moment, opened them again, gave her a long, tender look.

'Cherry,' he said. 'Heaven knows I believe you. If you fooled me, if you allowed any other chap to touch you, kiss you, I'd go mad, I'd kill you.' He gritted his teeth. 'You don't maybe realise what a love a girl like you can arouse in a fellow, Cherry,' he added. 'Darling, maybe you don't understand how murderous I'd feel if you were unfaithful to me.'

The next moment he was holding her in his arms, begging her to forgive him for imagining she would allow another to make love to her. His arms were enfolding her, his lips lingering on hers, and she hid her face against his shoulder and bit her lip. It was wonderful to think that she held a handsome, splendid man like this, that she could make him feel about her so intensely. For whatever happened then, and whatever the future held for her, she knew she could never love anyone like she loved Bill.

Later, when Cherry left Bill, he was thoroughly assured that she had never been disloyal to him in thought, word, or deed. She hurried back to the Manor House, thrilled and exultant. Before she said goodnight to Bill she had told him that she was applying to Lady Bayfield for a few days' holiday, as she was feeling over-worked and strained, owing to hard weeks of service in the hot weather. She had told him she was going to Brighton to stay with her aunt, Mrs. Orton, who lived there. And that had worked out most satisfactorily because Bill, in his turn, had informed her that he was going away for a day or two — to London first, then back to Little Cross.

When she asked him, rather uneasily, why he was going to London, he reassured her by saying that it was a wonderful secret, and that he wouldn't tell her unless it came off. Anyhow, he was going to the East End to one of these boxing training centres, so she wouldn't be likely to meet him in the West End, where she was to be married to Phillip.

From what Bill said, she guessed he had some scheme on about being trained for a boxing championship, and that a promoter who had heard about him was fixing up a meeting between Bill and a famous boxing coach. Well, good luck to it, she said. She would like to see Bill at the top of the tree.

They agreed they wouldn't see each other for a few days, and that she was to let Bill know when she returned from Brighton. Fortunately he didn't want to write to her. He wasn't a good correspondent — hated letter-writing. That served her purpose all right. She had no idea where Phillip meant to take her after the wedding, and she was sure it wouldn't be at all convenient to give any stated address for letters.

3

That next morning; Cherry had a part to play, and not very much time to play it. She was due to join Phillip in London some time during the morning, and was confidently expecting that she would find an express letter at her cottage-home, with his instructions.

She complained to Mrs. Odham, the cook housekeeper that she felt ill, as soon as she awoke. Mrs. Odham told her ladyship.

Now, Lady Bayfield was a very kind woman, noted for her niceness to her domestic staff, and as soon as she heard that Cherry was not well, she sent for her.

'What is the matter, Cherry?' she asked kindly.

Cherry put a hand to her head and complained of giddiness and general slackness.

'I think I need a few days' holiday, your ladyship, if you could spare me,' she said meekly. 'I'm not very strong, and this heat does upset me.'

'By all means take a few days off, Cherry,' was her gracious reply.

As soon as Cherry got home she rushed to the kitchen where her mother was washing out clothes in the copper.

'Mum, I've got a holiday,' she said breathlessly. 'I'm not well, and I'm going to Brighton at once, to stay a night or so with Aunt Kate. Is there a letter for me?'

Her mother wiped the soapsuds from her hands and looked at her with a rather pathetic sort of wonder in her faded eyes.

'Yes, Cherry — on the mantelpiece — an express one, with the London post-mark.'

Her heart leaped.

'Oh, that's about a new situation,' she said.

'I may be going up to town into another job.'

Her mother followed her into the stuffy little parlour, and plied her with questions while she read her letter. Her attention was riveted on it. She managed to conceal the crisp Bank of England notes which Phillip had put in his missive. But she was wildly thrilled by the sight of them. Fifty pounds — to her a small fortune; to him, a mere nothing. This was the beginning of her triumph. The letter, written from Phillip's club, instructed her to meet him at 12 o'clock, at Marylebone Registry Office. He had the ring, and a special licence. He would tell her more when they met, and she wasn't to buy any clothes — just to go up in her best. He would buy her trousseau afterwards.

Cherry shook with excitement. She could scarcely speak to her mother. But she looked at her watch and saw that it was half-past ten. She only had time to catch the eleven o'clock fast train to Victoria.

All the way up to London she kept thinking of the fact that she was going to be Mrs. Bellairs before the day ended. She had to force herself not to think about Bill. If she had allowed her thoughts of Bill to master her she could never have met and married Phillip that day.

Cherry disliked her best blue suit, white cotton blouse and cheap hat. But Phillip had promised to buy her trousseau after their wedding, so she consoled herself.

Once she was at the registry office, she had such a pink colour, and her eyes were so brilliant, that she looked strikingly pretty, in spite of her shabby clothes. She saw the love leap into Phillip's eyes when he met her. He was already there, waiting, and very smart he looked, in his grey suit, with a pale pink carnation in the buttonhole — a real bridegroom.

He seized both her hands.

'Cherry-ripe!'

She caught her breath and tried to laugh.

'It's mad — we're both mad, Phillip.'

'A sweet madness,' he said. 'My bride — actually my bride! I'd rather have this marriage with you than a wedding at St. George's with Veronica.'

And then they were married. Yes, Cherry Brown became Cherry Bellairs. A slender platinum circle, set with brilliants, was slipped on to her marriage-finger. She felt dizzy with excitement, and the heat of that office as she signed her maiden-name.

Then Cherry found herself in a great Daimler saloon, driven by a smart chauffeur — hired for the occasion — leaving the registry office behind her. She suddenly felt an awful sensation of fear — of the trapped bird in the gilded cage. She had flown deliberately into that cage; but she was in it all the same. She no longer belonged to herself, but to Phillip. And somehow, she could not stop thinking of Bill — she was haunted by the vision of his handsome face, of his overwhelming love for her; his jealousy; his faith. She had betrayed that faith and was the wife of another man. While Bill strove to achieve his ambition for her sake, she had given herself into the keeping of a man whom she did not really love.

She hid her face in her hands. She felt Phillip's arms go round her.

'Cherry, darling — what is it? You're married to me now. You don't regret it? You're not cross because it's a secret? I'd give a lot to acknowledge you, but I daren't — till my father dies. I depend on him for my cash, and I want such a lot — to spend on you, Cherry. You do understand, don't you?'

She answered incoherently. She wasn't thinking about the secrecy of the affair; only of Bill, whom she loved. She wouldn't like to have confessed to this man, who was now her husband, just how much she wished Bill were in his shoes to-day.

Phillip forced her to look up at him. She could have screamed. Her nerves were all on edge, her thoughts not in the least what the thoughts of a bride should have been.

However, Cherry kept her head, and Phillip never guessed the mental conflict which had harassed her. And the next hour or two with him restored her good humour, and self confidence. She did exactly what she had always longed to do, she bought clothes, shoes, hats, as many as she wanted, and without regard for price.

It amused Cherry's husband to take her to Hartnell and change her from a shabby girl into a fashionable woman — Mrs. Bellairs.

They went from one expensive shop to another. With pride Cherry listened to the soft flattery of the men and women who sold the latest models to her. They all said she looked marvellous.

There was a proud light too, in Phillip's dark eyes when he looked at her at the end of that shopping expedition. She would never forget that day when she stood in front of a long mirror in a very chic salon, admiring her new looks.

From head to toe she was exquisite, radiant. The various artists of the West End shops had done their work well, and Phillip willingly paid the huge bills, one after the other.

All her old, cheap things had been cast aside. She wore wonderful chiffon and lace lingerie, sheer Dupont stockings — tiny suede shoes. A perfect three-piece in tie-silk, turquoise, blue or black. A smart tailored coat — a tiny feathered cap. Phillip was proud of her.

'You look divine!' he exclaimed.

They emerged from the salon into the sunlit street, and into the big car again. Then they went to Carrier's in Bond Street; there she chose a necklace of milky pearls and a great diamond and emerald ring. After that, Arden's to buy huge bottles of scent, perfumed bath-powders and salts, face powders and creams — all the feminine things she had longed for.

It seemed all too good to be true, and in the wild thrill of it she forgot Bill and her broken vows.

Phillip suggested that they should go to a certain fashionable hotel on the river, at Maidenhead, for dinner, and the night. After that they were to fly over to Paris and spend two days there, doing the night clubs and some more shopping.

Cherry was filled with excitement. Paris — the gay city of any woman's dreams — more clothes, more thrills!

Alas for Bill! After that first feeling of uneasiness, after the marriage ceremony, had departed, Cherry gave herself wholly up to the rapture of her secret marriage with a wealthy young man. Her head was spinning with the excitement and novelty of money to burn, and the adornment of her beauty — and what wonder?

Phillip was very much in love with Cherry and at her command during those first hours of their marriage; and she tried to be extra charming to him just to show how pleased she was with life as his wife. She agreed with him that it would be wise to go about under an assumed name, in case he met any of his parents' friends, so they called themselves Mr. and Mrs. Gerard.

Once again during that thrilling day the memory of Bill came back to her, and she felt as though she would gladly back out of this marriage and rush away from Phillip. That was when she was sitting in front of the dressing-table brushing her hair. She looked at her reflection in the mirror — such a slim, beautiful girl, in a nightgown of white chiffon and a dressing-gown which Phillip had chosen of ivory velvet, with a satin collar and cuffs. Silky brown head glistening in the electric light; cheeks flushed; hazel eyes luminous, bright with triumph. Around her a luxurious room, full of extravagant clothes and downstairs a wonderful wedding-dinner had been specially ordered, and her in a silver gown, the cynosure of all eyes in the restaurant. What more could she want? What more had she dreamed of?

But she knew what troubled her. The one thing missing was Bill. If Bill had been her husband — if his had been those footsteps which she heard in the corridor, what rapture then!

Cherry's reflection in the mirror paled, the hand half hidden by a big cuff was cold.

In answer to a gentle tapping on the door she heard herself say:

'Come in!'

Then her husband came across the room, and the next moment she was in his arms.

For a few days she was happy, and thrilled by the novelty of everything, and her mind, so full really of Bill, became drugged by sheer excitement.

The trip by plane from Northolt to Le Bourget was wonderful. Cherry adored Paris. Phillip showered her with gifts. She was taken to shows, shops in the Rue de la Paix, where there were dresses, hats and lingerie to make a woman's mouth water.

But after three days of that feverish

exotic life she was forced — and Phillip was forced, too — to return to practical thought.

Phillip had business in town to attend to, and Cherry had to return to Dalescombe in order to prevent suspicion arising in the mind of her family — and particularly to prevent any trouble with Bill. She had not yet told Phillip a word about Bill. She felt she must see him and deal tactfully with the situation.

They flew back to London. Phillip got Cherry a furnished service flat in the vicinity of Grosvenor Square.

'You can leave all your luggage there, Cherry, and have the key, and get away, when you can, to see me,' he said. 'You must send in notice to Lady Bayfield and tell your people you're going to a job in town.'

'I've already paved the way for that,' she said. 'My job will be personal maid to — Mrs. Gerard, eh?'

'Yes, and Mrs. Gerard is a very beautiful, fascinating woman, and Mr.

Gerard is wildly in love with her,' said her husband, laughing and kissing her passionately.

Cherry was worn out with the excitement and fatigue of Paris, and Phillip's kisses never really thrilled her like Bill's did. She was not in a very good humour either. It did not appeal to her to have to discard her beautiful clothes; leave them behind her, and go back to her home as Cherry Brown.

But it had to be done, and Phillip had business on hand.

He saw her into a train.

An hour later she was in Dalescombe. 'Mrs. Gerard' turned back into Cherry Brown.

She hadn't been home half an hour before Bill rode over on his cycle from Little Cross to see her.

Her mother, believing that Bill Carew was courting Cherry, left them alone in the lounge, and there Bill caught her in his arms.

'Cherry, my dear — such news for

you!' were his first words. 'Wonderful news — all the more wonderful because it is for you.'

She stared up at him and said:

'What is it, Bill? What has happened?'

Before he answered her he kissed her.

'You smell of — oh, of flowers; some gorgeous sort of scent, Cherry, darling! What is it?'

'Oh, something I got in Brighton for a treat!' she said. But she thought of the gilded perfume shop in Paris, where Phillip had bought the perfume. 'But tell me what has happened?' she said impatiently.

Bill sat down in a rocking-chair which had belonged to her grandmother, and drew her down beside him. She couldn't help feeling thrilled as she laid her head on his shoulder.

He told her his news. He had met a big promoter in London — and also a famous trainer — Joe Wilson, who had trained some of the finest middle-weights in Britain — and another man, called Henry Frinton, who was a manager. Frinton himself had seen Bill box in some village contest, and realised he had the makings of a champion.

'And now, Cherry, it's all settled,' Bill finished excitedly. 'I'm to start training at once, under Joe Wilson, and Frinton is to be my manager. Cherry, it's my great chance. I can throw up the rotten garage job in Little Cross. I shall train now to meet the present middle-weight champion and, if I succeed, I shall be rich — rich enough to marry you, Cherry, and give you all you deserve.'

She listened to him with a sinking heart. In one way she was terribly pleased that his chance had come. In another, she was furious — furious with herself for marrying Phillip. If she had not been so greedy, so ambitious, if she had waited, she might have married the man whom she really, truly loved and had wanted.

However, Cherry tried to show Bill that she was delighted, and to share his enthusiasm and excitement. He was full of gratitude to the promoter who was financing his training.

'I'd do anything to show him how grateful I am, Cherry, and to-morrow night he is coming down to the King's Arms, at Little Cross, to have some dinner along with me and Joe Wilson and my manager, Frinton. I'm to put on the gloves and give the boss a little exhibition of what I can do. You're to come. I've told Mr. Frinton I've got a sweetheart, and he said you might come but that I wasn't to get married till after my training, and I'd shown the world what I'm made of.'

Cherry tried to forget Phillip and their marriage. She grew thrilled and interested in Bill's wonderful news and the dinner in Little Cross to-morrow. She was always happy in the company of men, and she didn't doubt Bill's backer and the other two would admire Bill's taste in a girlfriend.

So that next night, to please Bill, she put on a white cotton frock, pinned a couple of pink roses on her shoulder, and looking like any country girl going out with her boy friend, she waited for Bill to cycle over from Little Cross and fetch her. She had an old bicycle too, and was going to ride with him. She, who had lately ridden in a Daimler saloon. It was a queer situation, and Phillip, her lovely jewels and clothes seemed far off that night.

When Bill and Cherry were cycling side by side, his arm about her shoulders, on the road from Dalescombe to Little Cross, he gave her a queer, sheepish look.

'Cherry, I've got a surprising bit of news for you.'

'What's that?' she smiled at him.

'Well, Mr. Frinton wrote to me and told me the name of my unknown backer. You could have knocked me down with a feather when I read it!'

'What was it?' she asked.

'Why, nobody but your old flame,' he said in a teasing voice.

'My old flame?' she repeated, puzzled.

'I'm only ragging you, sweetheart.'

Her heart gave a leap, and the front wheel of her bike swerved dangerously.

'Bill, who is it?' she gasped.

'Mr. Bellairs, Cherry. It's him you and I will be dining with tonight.'

She did not answer Bill for some time. She cycled along mechanically, hardly seeing the road before her. She was in the grip of sheer terror. Phillip was the man who was going to finance this training as a boxer — her husband! She wondered if the beating of the pulse in her head would stop. What could she do now?

Cherry knew she dared not go on to Little Cross with Bill and come face to face with Phillip. He would give the show away at once. He would be madly jealous and astonished that Bill should be calling her his girlfriend and introducing her to the others as his future wife. But, if Bill guessed for a single moment that she had deceived him so terribly there would be bloodshed. That she did not doubt. She knew how angry Bill could be. She shivered as she thought of that night by Dalescombe Woods when he had sworn to kill her if she were faithless to him — kill the man too!

Cherry dared not risk such catastrophies, she thought as they cycled along, her knees growing weaker and weaker. She must pretend to be ill, do something desperate — anything to prevent this awful meeting at the King's Arms.

Bill was saying:

'You're not cross that I've accepted Mr. Bellairs' offer, darling? It was too big a temptation — if he felt he wanted to finance me. I'll pay him back, you can be sure, when I'm middle-weight champion!'

She muttered some unintelligible reply. She said to herself:

'Phillip mustn't see me with Bill tonight. Bill must not know about Phillip.'

Then she gave a little cry and rocked on her cycle.

'Bill, Bill!' she gasped.

'Good Heavens, Cherry! What is it?' he exclaimed. And he jumped off his machine and let it crash to the road, putting both arms about her swaying figure. He looked up at her and immediately said: 'You are ill — you've gone a ghastly colour. Tell me, what is it?'

She let him help her off the bike and leaned heavily against him. He put a supporting arm about her. She clapped both hands to her head.

'My head,' she moaned. 'Such pain! I felt rotten at home, but I didn't want to tell you, dear — to spoil our evening. I think I'm in the grip of 'flu or something. Oh, Bill, I do feel so bad!'

He smoothed the hair back from her face and took her hand, and gazed anxiously down at her.

'My poor little girl! You're burning — you must have a temperature. Oh, Cherry, honey, why didn't you tell me before we started? I'd never have let you come out on your bike like this with a fever, if I'd known.'

Cherry shut her eyes. She was near to tears.

'You must go on to the meeting. You mustn't keep them waiting, darling,' she muttered. 'Look, here's Farmer Jupp coming along in his car. He'll give me and my bike a lift home.'

'Certainly not! I shall come with you!' said Bill warmly. 'I wouldn't dream of leaving you if you're sick. But Cherry, darling, won't the headache pass? Couldn't you possibly come on? I did so want you to meet everyone. I simply can't understand it — you were so well and gay when we left the cottage.' And he looked at her with bewildered, puzzled eyes.

Cherry felt very remorseful. She had to go on with the game for both their sakes. She let the tears trickle down her cheeks.

'I'm so sorry, Bill. I hoped I'd feel better if I set out; but now I'm worse. I simply couldn't face meeting anyone, and a noisy supper. Farmer Jupp will take me home.'

Bill looked down the road. A grey-haired man whom they both knew — he kept a farm between Little Cross and Dalescombe — was driving slowly along in his car.

'Darling, I'll come with you — ' began Bill.

'Nonsense!' Cherry interrupted him, trying to speak cheerfully. 'It wouldn't do for you to miss your appointment, and it's getting late now. I'm perfectly all right. Mr. Jupp will see me home safely.'

Bill caught her close to him — kissed her with great tenderness.

'I don't like to leave you. Why, you're crying! You must be feeling awfully bad. Poor sweetie.'

The thought of Phillip haunted and worried her. Why had she married him? Why was she deceiving Bill shamefully? Why?

The answer was, of course, because she wanted what Phillip's money could buy. But if she had waited — if Bill became a boxing champion — he, too, would be rich. What folly she had committed!

She found herself driven back to her home in the car beside Mr. Jupp. She was silent, sullen, tearing her handkerchief to shreds in her lap with nervous fingers. She had sent Bill off fairly cheerful, and certain that she had the 'flu and could not accompany him. He had cautioned her to go to bed at once, and said he would call to see her in the morning. He had been adorable.

And here she was, well and strong, flushed with temper and not fever, having to go back to the cottage and miss a gay party at Little Cross because the man financing Bill was her husband!

'What be you doin' gettin' sick, Cherry?' old Farmer Jupp was asking her in a friendly fashion. 'It's too bad, an' you missin' a treat up at Little Cross an' all.'

She answered him in a non-committal fashion. He was a talkative old chap, and began to launch into stories of the bad wheat crop and the lack of sunshine; lamenting the loss of lambs back in the spring, and the price of labour in the future. She let him speak on, hardly heard what he said. She was thinking of that supper at the King's Arms.

Bill — what Bill would say to his benefactor. Would he mention her name? That was a dread, a terror. What if Bill suggested to Phillip that he was engaged to her? But she didn't, somehow, think that her name would come into the conversation. Surely it would be purely a business talk — all boxing. And she knew, as a general rule, if Bill spoke of her, it was as his girlfriend, one of the Brown family. That might mean any one of her sisters. And there were other Browns in the village. Phillip wouldn't for a moment suspect that she was Bill's girlfriend. At least, she banked on the fact that he wouldn't, and that Bill wouldn't give away particulars. He was discreet and, like most men, not too ready with information about his private affairs.

Anyhow, it can well be imagined that Cherry spent that evening at home worrying, wondering, haunted by all sorts of fears.

Old Farmer Jupp dropped her and her cycle at home, and her mother and sister Polly put her to bed, quite worried about her health, and suggested that Dr. Webster from the village should be sent for at once. But Cherry pooh-poohed this. She knew the doctor would see through her, find her temperature quite normal, and her headache a sham. She told her family she would be all right in the morning and begged them to leave her alone.

Her mother switched off the light and left her in bed in darkness. But the moment she had gone Cherry crept out of bed and sat by the open window, staring at the moon-silvered fields around their cottage, biting her lips, restless, tortured by anxiety. She felt she could not sleep a wink until she was sure Bill had given nothing away to Phillip. She was quite certain Phillip wouldn't give away his news! He was much too keen to keep their marriage a secret.

Half the night she crouched by the bedroom window, growing cold and shivery. But she was unconscious of her chilled limbs. Her hot bed would have stifled her and she wanted to think. And the more she thought the more depressed she became. This new relationship between Bill and Phillip complicated matters horribly. Bill might see Phillip often. She would never be at peace while they were meeting. At any second one of them might give her away, say something that would. She thought of the exotic, feverish, luxurious days of her honeymoon; of her smart clothes. They mattered — quite a lot. She still adored what money could buy. And as Phillip was, at the moment, the man of wealth, he still had a certain

64

fascination for her. She made up her mind to keep them both — the man she had married and the man she loved.

It was a dreadful thing for a girl to contemplate; but Cherry thought that she could not live without the love of Bill any more than she had been able to overcome the irresistible lure of her husband's money.

And while one part of her knew a sense of satisfaction at the wealth she had at her command, there was another, stronger side that was calling: 'Bill — my Bill, I want you!'

4

Morning came.

Cherry had had such a bad night and so little sleep that she really looked ill in the daylight. Her face was pale and haggard. There were dark lines under her eyes. But she was cool and collected again and assured her mother that her temperature had gone down and that it had only been a slight feverish attack soon over.

'Bill may come in to see me,' Cherry informed her mother carelessly. 'If he does — show him up.'

'Come now, Cherry,' said her mother in her prim fashion. 'It isn't the thing for a young girl like you receiving a fellow in her bedroom.'

Cherry felt like telling her to be quiet, the silly old-fashioned thing. As if Cherry were shy and scared of the idea of a man being in her bedroom. Cherry had never been like that. In her way she was as fiercely reserved and innocent as any of her less experienced sisters, but she hadn't any artificial stupid feeling of mock-modesty. To her it would be quite natural for Bill to come up and sit on her bed and she knew he wouldn't see any wrong in it, either. He was much too decent and clean-minded. She felt contemptuous of those who see evil in everything.

She didn't argue with her mother. She simply said:

'Don't be silly, mum, I haven't just left school.'

And after she had walked off, talking about the 'fast ways of the modern girl', Cherry lay back on her pillow, thinking of Phillip. My goodness, what would poor old mum have said if she could have known that her Cherry was already a married woman ... Mrs. Phillip Bellairs.

Bill came up to see her. She knew that he would ... tiptoeing into her room as though it were a sacred shrine holding the presence of his beloved. He was really rather adorable. He sat down on her bed and took both her small slim hands and covered them with kisses.

'Angel — Cherry — are you better?'

Her heart gave a throb of utter relief. She knew at once that nothing had gone wrong; that nothing had been said at The Kings Arms last night to give her away.

She felt so elated, so happy, she wanted to fling herself into Bill's arms — cover his brown, handsome face with kisses. But she controlled the desire. She knew what high ideals Bill had about women. She thought she had better play the part of the shy young girl, anyhow. So she just let him kiss her hands and whispered:

'I feel much better, Bill. In fact I shall get up after lunch. It was a funny attack — didn't last long. I felt very ill when I got home.'

'You still look pale, mavourneen,' he said, his Irish eyes tender with anxiety.

'Sure you oughtn't to have the doc?'

'Certain,' Cherry said. 'Tell me about last night.'

'Oh, it went off jolly well, Cherry.'

Holding her hands, kissing them at intervals, he launched into a graphic description of the meeting between the promoter; the manager; the trainer and himself. Mr. Bellairs, he said, had been most sporting and ready to do what he could. He, Bill, had to put on the gloves and had one or two rounds with Joe Wilson — knocked the trainer out, too! Bellairs had been delighted and they were all sure they had got a winner in him.

Bill puffed out his deep chest proudly.

'Reckon I might win the middle-weight championship of the world, one day, Cherry, and by jingo, what a day for me . . . with you as my wife. I'll be a Randolph Turpin, see if I don't.'

She shivered and turned her eyes from his glowing face.

'I'm mad,' she thought. 'Why didn't I

wait . . . what a crazy fool I've been!'

'Just you see, Cherry,' continued Bill. 'A few months' training . . . and I'll knock down all the Sugar Ray Robinsons. But I'm getting conceited — puffed out with pride after what they said about me last night,' and he laughed . . . in reality a very modest man, boyishly elated by his triumphs. Cherry thought him very charming. She put his hand against her cheek; kissed his strong brown fingers.

'Oh, I do love you!' she whispered.

He slid on to his knees by her bed and laid his curly head against the curve of her hip.

'Darling Cherry. Everything will be for you — every bit of work — all the success — for you, darling.'

Her throat felt dry. She could have sobbed. Then he looked up at her, his eyes warm and passionate. He leaned down and pressed a lingering kiss on her parted lips.

'I love you too,' he whispered. 'Cherry, I mustn't stay up here. I'm going down right now.'

She didn't argue with him. She dared not. With all her heart she wanted to wind her arms about his neck and abandon herself to love. She let him get up and walk away from her. At the door he turned and gave her a most attractive smile.

'Hang it, I'd be so jealous if any other fellow so much as set foot in this room, Cherry, I'd shoot him,' he said.

'You silly!' she laughed uneasily.

But her cheeks flamed crimson. What —WHAT would Bill say if he knew the truth . . . knew that Phillip Bellairs of whom he had just been speaking with respect and liking, had been to Paris with Cherry . . . was her *husband* . . . had the right to walk into her room and stay there. She turned her face to the pillow, loathing herself because of the faith in Bill's eyes, and the respect in which he held her.

Just as he was going, she called him back.

'Bill, darling — '

Eagerly he looked at her from the doorway.

'Yes, darling.'

'Did you — mention about your engagement when you were with Mr. Bellairs?'

'No,' he said. 'I wanted to. I'm so proud of you, Cherry. But Mr. Wilson and Mr. Frinton both said it wasn't a good thing for a boxer to have his head full of a love-affair and that Mr. Bellairs would prefer to think of me as unattached with my mind right on my training. So I'm keeping our engagement a secret. Then, as soon as I've shown the world what I can do and won a bit of money, I can marry you, Cherry.'

She sighed with relief. That was splendid. Nothing could be better. In a casual voice she said:

'By the way, Bill, I'm leaving the Manor House.'

'Why?' asked Bill, astonished. 'It is the best job you've had, isn't it? You like her Ladyship and they pay you three quid a week.'

'I know. But Bill — ' she cleared her throat and tried to look him in the eye. 'Dalescombe doesn't suit me. I've had one or two funny attacks lately and I've decided that London air might suit me best. I've written to an agency up there and had some good offers and I — I've taken a post in town.'

'You've taken one?' he exclaimed, staring at her with mild curiosity. 'You funny little thing — you never mentioned it to me.'

'I was waiting till it was settled.'

'Well, and what have you got, darling?' he asked, smiling at her in his charming way.

'A very good job,' Cherry lied. 'As personal maid to a Mrs. Gerard in Grosvenor Square.'

'Sounds grand,' said Bill. 'But are you sure it's all right? I don't want you going to some place in London you know nothing about. You're so young and inexperienced, Cherry.'

She bit her lip impatiently.

'I'm all right, Bill. Mrs. Gerard is — very nice . . . ' She couldn't help laughing at her own irony. Taking the job as 'personal maid' to herself. It was really amusing. 'I'm starting with her on Monday next.'

'Well, I hope you won't have to do a domestic job much longer, Cherry,' he said, his handsome eyes caressing her. 'I'm just living for the day when you and I can get married.'

'Darling,' she said (What else *could* she say. Her heart was full of love for him — desire and longing and some remorse).

'If it comes to that, I'm not sorry you've taken a job in town, Cherry,' he added. 'I'm going tomorrow to Wilson's place in Tunbridge Wells and we are likely to pop up from there to town to his other place in Hammersmith quite often so whenever I'm there I can see you.'

Swiftly Cherry told herself that it could be arranged — somehow — with great discretion although it would always be very dangerous, and when Bill asked for her address with 'Mrs. Gerard' she gave it boldly.

'Don't go there to see me without writing,' she murmured, 'and don't phone. Mrs. Gerard mightn't like it. You can write — Miss Brown, c/o Mrs. Gerard, 31 Connor Court, Grosvenor Square.'

He wrote it down on a scrap of paper in his pocket; returned to give the slim girl a final kiss and went off saying:

'I'll see you before I go away, darling. Hurry up and get better.'

Cherry was 'much better' later that day. By the following day was quite herself again in the eyes of the family. She had said good-bye to Bill . . . he had gone . . . left Little Cross bearing the good wishes of his many friends, to train with Wilson under Frinton's management. Everybody in Dalescombe was talking of him . . . what a fine boxer he was . . . what a grand chance he had of becoming a champion. Cherry listened, silent and thoughtful, feeling proud ... proud that this wonderful young man was in love with her — knowing that she held him in the hollow of her hand.

Then she heard something that amused her in a malicious way. It was common gossip that Miss Bayfield of the Manor House, was inconsolable because her fiancé had jilted her. Nobody knew why, but Mr. Bellairs had broken his engagement. Lady Bayfield was furious. Veronica was left lamenting. At the same time Cherry heard that the Bayfields were shutting up the Manor House and going over to Le Touquet (where Veronica was to find consolation, poor, silly, girl!) That made it much easier for Cherry to give immediate notice to her ladyship. Her notice was accepted; quite graciously; she was given a month's salary and told her family that she was off to town to be a personal maid to 'Mrs. Gerard'.

It never entered anybody's head to doubt the situation.

Two days later Cherry was back in

her luxurious flat. She engaged an excellent cook-housekeeper and a daily maid. She changed like a chameleon in these surroundings. She ceased to be Cherry Brown. She became the beautiful, smart, glamorous 'Mrs. Gerard'. She wrote to Phillip at his Club, informing him that she was back in town and waited for him to come to her.

One fine September afternoon, she sat in her bedroom in a deep armchair; a gold satin cushion behind her chestnut head; her feet in blue satin sandals; her slim figure looked perfect in a black Chantilly lace housecoat — the lace like a film over pale blue silk — a wide blue sash confining her tiny waist.

Her room which had been furnished to suit her taste, was charming; powder-blue carpet; blue satin curtains framing gossamer transparent net; the windows over-looked the green Square, and Roosevelt's statue. She could watch the big expensive cars moving constantly around and felt thrilled because she was 'Mrs. Gerard' and in a position to own a car just as big and expensive as any she saw. Her furniture was Louis Quinze — a delicate white and gilt French suite; her bed a big double divan with a head-board of studded blue satin. On a little table beside the bed stood a Venetian glass vase of red carnations; some of the latest novels from the Times Book Club, a box of chocolates; the new Tatler and Sketch. Her dressing-table was littered with scent-bottles; powder-bowls; creams and lotions; all the most expensive cosmetics. Cherry revelled in the luxury and beauty of it all. She stretched herself out in her low chair and idled away the afternoon with an exciting book, and a little white radio. This was a thousand times better than life in Dalescombe; better than life with poor Bill could ever have been. Yet she wanted Bill. She would have given all these things to have known that this flat; these expensive toys; and she herself, belonged to her first love.

She gave only a careless thought to her husband. He had not been in when she phoned and had not yet telephoned to her. He was being a bit casual. She really was rather puzzled by his conduct. Surely he was not tired of her already? Men did not tire easily of Cherry Brown. *Yet where was he?*

She flung aside her book. It was highbrow and it bored her. In her heart of hearts she wished she had her 'Home Notes' or 'Picture Post'. She could understand them. The papers her mother took in regularly; stories to suit her intelligence which did not run to serious psychological or intellectual literature.

She walked to the window: drummed her fingers on the pane, yawned.

'Where on earth is Phillip?' she reflected.

Then her heart gave a tremendous jolt. For a taxi had just rolled around the Square and drawn up before the block in which Cherry's flat was situated. Out of that taxi stepped a tall young man; brown, handsome, eager, wearing grey flannels and a soft green hat. It was Bill. Bill had disobeyed her . . . come to call without letting her know and here she was in her lace nightie — Mrs. Gerard; her housekeeper and daily maid both in. *What would he say?* How could she keep the truth from him now?'

5

Never before had Cherry been so frightened. Her heart pounded. She shook from head to foot. She felt her face burn; then grow cold and white.

But she knew it was useless to stand there staring out of the window. She must act at once.

She caught at the delicate Chantilly lace of her negligee, tearing it in her nervousness. She rushed from the drawing-room along the corridor of her little flat to her housekeeper's room. She called hoarsely to the young Hungarian 'daily', who was in there, talking to the cook.

'Anna, Anna!'

'Yes, Madam,' came the answer and the door half-opened. Fortunately Anna was changing from her coloured overall into her dark blue silk dress and coffee-coloured organdie apron; her

81

hair was up in kirby-grips and she was far from ready to answer a front-door bell. She was a nice girl — quiet and smart at her work and already adored Cherry who could be charming and sympathetic to women as well as men. She was particularly nice to those in her employ, remembering her own days as a 'domestic'. Both the housekeeper and Anna who had only been with Cherry a week, would do any mortal thing for her.

'Anna,' Cherry said breathlessly, smiling at her, although she felt like weeping, she was so worried about Bill. 'Be a good girl and lend me one of your overalls and give me a dustpan and brush.'

Anna's eyes opened wide. Cherry hastened to concoct her story.

'You see, Anna, I am going to a fancy-dress dance this week-end and I think I'll go as a 'daily'. The gentleman I'm going with is just coming up to see me now, so I want to show him what I shall look like. He might go as an old-fashioned butler, with side-whiskers. It will be fun, won't it?' And Cherry giggled, stupidly.

Anna never suspected a lie; neither did she think Cherry's manner strange or noticed her burning cheeks and brilliant, excited eyes. She was all too pleased to help Cherry with her 'fancy-dress' and thought it amusing as she handed her the overall and the dustpan and brush.

'It is a clean one, madam. My word! You will look sweet in it, if I may say so. You are sweet in anything,' she said with her strong Hungarian accent.

Cherry grabbed the things, made some laughing reply, then rushed to her bedroom. She tore off the black lace; the satin mules; put on some court shoes; Anna's white overall; tied a scarf over her hair.

The front-door bell was ringing. Bill must have been ringing it for two solid minutes. In a moment he would go away, or Anna would take it upon herself to open the door. Cherry's hands shook so that she could scarcely tie the scarf over her head. As she looked at herself in her glass, she reflected grimly that the uniform did suit her. Little did Anna know how accustomed the beautiful 'Mrs. Gerard' was to a servant's uniform.

At last she was ready. She rushed to the front door and opened it. She breathed so fast she nearly choked as she looked up at the man she loved.

'Good-afternoon, Sir,' she said demurely.

Bill gave her an eager, devouring glance — the glance of an adoring lover — swept off his hat and seized her in his great arms, almost knocking the dustpan and brush from her hand.

'Cherry — angel,' he breathed.

'Ssh,' she said, with a finger to her lips, 'Mrs. Gerard is resting. She mustn't hear . . . '

Bill's lips brushed her mouth . . . then lingered in a kiss of deep, intense passion.

'Lovely, lovely Cherry — my dearest,' he crooned in his beguiling voice which, to Cherry, always held all the haunting, seductive beauty of Ireland. 'I don't care who hears. I only know I love you and have been dying to see you, darling.'

She drew away from him, breathless with emotion. His fierce embrace had left her trembling.

'You are a one,' she whispered. 'Didn't I tell you not to come without letting me know?'

'Forgive me, darling, but I got a day's holiday suddenly and I just had to rush to you while I got the chance.'

'You could have phoned.'

He looked at her with a smile, half-apologetic, half-amused.

'Cross with me, angel?'

'You know I'm not. But — Mrs. Gerard is particular about her staff. She's liable to wake up and call for her tea any moment now. I must go back. I daren't stay and talk to you.'

His handsome face clouded.

'Oh, Cherry!'

'I know, it's a shame, but this is a good job and I don't want to lose it. Mrs. Gerard won't allow her maids to have young men.'

Cherry was thoroughly amused because the danger had passed and Bill was quite taken in by her appearance. He looked at her overall and her demure head scarf, concealing the nut brown curls he loved.

'Darling little maid,' he said tenderly. 'You look enchanting, though I hate you working for anybody.'

'I'm very happy,' she said, biting her lip.

He caught her in his arms, again, having first cast a furtive glance around to make sure nobody was about.

'Kiss me, Cherry. I love you so.'

She yielded to his arms for a moment, her eyes closing. Just for a few seconds she hated the lies and the deception and the intrigue of it all. She wished she really was a servant in the flat; that no Phillip existed; that she could welcome her Bill with a clear conscience and a pure heart. She knew that she was behaving outrageously. Yet she was not wholly bad. In Bill's arms, surrendering to his kiss, she felt the tears prick her eyes; almost the yearning to break down and sob and confess her sins. She remembered when she was a child her mother saying:

'Never tell lies, Cherry. They do get you in awful scrapes, and God above knows.'

Yes — God alone knew what Cherry was doing and soon, if she went on with this dangerous game with two men, she might get into trouble. She was Phillip's wife and she loved Bill. She was bound to the two men by ties equally strong. She had to go on.

Cherry didn't want to send Bill away yet she dared not let him into the flat. Anna would think it strange if she continued to talk to a visitor in her overall and Phillip might turn up at any minute, now that he knew she was back. It would be disastrous if he found

Bill and Cherry together. She questioned Bill quickly about his affairs. He told her he was getting on marvellously. He looked 'fighting' fit; bronzed face, clear eyes; splendid shoulders erect. And he pulled up his sleeves and showed her the rippling muscles on his arms. Those wonderful biceps! She was thrilled and proud of her boxer.

'A regular champion already, dear, darling Bill,' she murmured, clinging to him.

'Oh, I will be one day,' he smiled self-consciously. 'Wilson is pleased with me, anyhow. Cherry, sweet, tomorrow I go down to Tunbridge Wells and I shall be training there for a fortnight. Today is my last chance of seeing you for two whole weeks. Do you think Mrs. Gerard would give you an evening off to come out with me?'

'Oh, no — I'm sure she wouldn't.'

'She must — you must explain — say it's your long-lost brother, anything,' he urged, smiling. 'Oh, Cherry, a whole two weeks before I see you again.

Angel, *do* come out — even after dinner — we'll go to the flicks. I've never taken you out in the West End of London. Do — do try!'

Cherry hesitated — and was lost. She longed to go out with him. Her heart sank at the thought of not seeing him for a whole fortnight. She did love him so. An evening with Bill . . . a simple happy evening . . . a domestic with her boyfriend. It would really mean more to her than any night at the opera or theatre with Phillip — any formal, sticky evening with his rich friends. At heart she was still Cherry Brown, although she tried to deceive herself into believing she liked to be glamorous Mrs. Bellairs. She did, too, feel that hopeless passion for money and all that it could buy.

She was sorely tempted to go out with Bill. Phillip had not come; had not written. She was feeling fed up with her newly-made husband. She had only a lonely, boring evening to look forward to. She gave way to Bill's pleading.

'Wait a second,' she said. 'I'll run and see if Mrs. Gerard is awake and I'll ask her.'

She ran into the bedroom; pretended to have a conversation with 'Mrs. Gerard' and ran back to Bill.

'It's O.K., darling. She says I may go out with my long-lost brother at seven o'clock as she is dining out unexpectedly.'

Bill's face looked radiant. He caught her close and kissed her eager mouth.

'Splendid. Then shall I call for you?'

'No, no,' she said hurriedly. 'I'll meet you out.'

'Right-oh. Corner of the street.'

'No,' Cherry said uneasily. 'Further away.'

'You're very nervous of being seen with me,' he remarked more in fun than anything, but Cherry went quite pale with anxiety. She hastened to assure him she was not, but that she'd rather meet him further afield. So they arranged to meet outside Oxford Circus Tube Station at 7.30.

'Then we'll have a lovely evening, darling. I'm quite well-off tonight. Wilson is very generous. I'll take you to eat at Lyons Corner House,' he said. He added: 'Thank Mrs. Gerard for letting you off, Cherry. She must be very considerate.'

'M'm,' muttered Cherry.

'What's she like? Is she good to you?'

'Very,' said Cherry, gulping, and turned a crimson face away from Bill. She felt mean and double-faced before his candour and simplicity. She was actually in tears when he had gone and she was back in her bedroom taking off the overall.

She stared angrily at her face in the mirror.

'Little fool,' she said viciously. 'What's the use of howling?'

She knew in her heart, that she would be just discontented and restive if she could turn back the hands of Time and find herself Cherry Brown again instead of rich Mrs. Bellairs. She had always been madly ambitious. And now she was Phillip's wife and had everything money could buy, but she felt mean and despicable.

The perversity of human nature! One always wanted what one couldn't get and when one got it, one didn't want it any more.

However, luxury and nice things were still too great a novelty to bore Cherry for long, and for half-an-hour after Bill had gone, she lay in a hot, steaming bath, fragrant and cloudy, delicately perfumed with bath-essence, and revelled in the joy of it. It was nice to be 'Mrs. Gerard,' really; nice to come out of that bath into a huge, soft Turkish towel, warm from lying on the hot rail; to shake scented bath-powder over her slim rosy body; to sit cosily wrapped in her white velvet wrapper, whilst Anna brushed her chestnut hair and set out fresh lingerie — mist grey chiffon, a satin slip and expensive belt and bra.

Then she told Anna to go. She didn't want her any more. She might think it queer of Cherry put on a plain suit for tonight's entertainment. She took off her pearls, her diamond earrings and clips, when she had gone and quickly dressed in her most simple grey suit and white shirt and a small flowered cap which would not rouse Bill's suspicions. He would not know how much the apparently simple things had cost Phillip.

Then, taking a plain bag and a pair of white chamois gloves, she started to walk along the passage to the front door. Her heart was singing softly: 'Bill . . . I love you.' She looked forward intensely to their evening together. Her blood leapt with the thrilling thought of his embrace . . . how he would hold her, kiss her. She could imagine him being extravagant and taking her home in a taxi for the pure pleasure of kissing her. Nobody's kisses were like Bill's. He was such a splendid lover.

Then Cherry stopped dead, in the hall, every drop of blood draining from her cheeks; a sick, sinking feeling in her heart.

Somebody was fitting a latch-key into the front-door. She knew who it was. It could be nobody else. Only one other person beside herself had a key to the flat.

Phillip walked in.

Phillip shut the door behind him and pocketed the key. He looked at Cherry somewhat casually, she thought.

'Oh, hullo, darling — so you are in!'

She couldn't speak. Heart pounding, throat dry. She leaned against the wall and stared at him, foolishly. She wondered desperately how she could keep her appointment with Bill, now that her husband had come home.

Phillip took off his coat and tossed it on to the hall-stand, then smoothed his hair off his forehead. Cherry thought his thin face looked a trifle haggard today and the lips under their dark line of moustache were sulky. He was not in a good temper. However, he came up to her and caught her in his arms.

'Seems ages since I saw you,

Cherry-ripe. How are you, pet?'

Somehow the touch of his arms suddenly revolted her. Her heart, her brain were full of Bill. It was to Bill she had been going like an ardent woman to her true love. She felt stone-cold in her husband's arms. When his lips — cold and sensual — touched Cherry's, she shrank away.

Phillip sensed her distaste and instantly released her. He was a proud, vain man and not one to brook reluctance on the part of the girl he had married.

He stared at Cherry, surprise and hostility in his gaze. She stared back; hostility in hers. For the first time they seemed aware of each other as enemies rather than passionate lovers secretly married and it was strange . . . rather terrifying to Cherry. Some change had come over both of them; she had definitely regretted her rash marriage since Bill had the chance of making money and she supposed Phillip regretted it, too . . . having got all he had wanted. Such is man, in the grip of satiety.

'What the hell is up with you, Cherry?' he asked bluntly.

She strove for composure and speech. She really did not know what to say or do for a moment. She realised that it would be a pity to quarrel with her husband. It would be quarreling with the golden goose, so to speak. On the other hand she was obsessed with the thought of Bill, waiting for her outside Oxford Circus Tube Station. A glance at her wristwatch showed her that it was twenty-five past seven. She could not let Bill know that 'Mr. Gerard' had returned, and that 'Mrs. Gerard' wanted her. How could she let him know? She dared not entrust any message to her maid. It would look so very funny. She dared not rouse their suspicions.

What could she do? She felt frantic, cornered. She tried to temporise, and said, in a low, trembling voice:

'You haven't treated me very well, Phillip, leaving me to myself all this week. I wrote to your Club — told you I was back.

He gave a short laugh.

'So that's it — you're piqued with me.'

'Don't be absurd,' Cherry said, stamping her foot. 'I am your wife. You're treating me as though I were your — '

'Steady, Cherry. Aren't you rocking the boat a bit?' he interrupted, frowning. 'You're annoyed because I've neglected you. I'm sorry. I've been extremely busy. When we parted, I told you I had some business on hand. As a matter of fact I'm financing a big boxing stunt if you want the truth and I've been tied up with that, on top of my duty visits to my family.'

She laughed grimly. She knew everything there was to know about that 'boxing stunt'. She wondered what Phillip would have said if she had informed him that she was just about to meet his protege — Bill Carew of Little Cross!

'You must be reasonable, Cherry,' Phillip continued. 'You know my people expect me to stay with them occasionally and that I'd be cut off without a bean if they guessed I was married to you. They're furious with me for breaking my engagement with Veronica. They considered that a decent match and wanted me to settle down . . . ' he gave a short laugh . . . 'I had to lie about it — say Veronica and I didn't agree.'

'Well, wasn't it true? Are you suggesting that you regret breaking with her? Are you sorry you married me?' Cherry demanded, shaking from head to foot. She felt suddenly, furiously angry with Phillip. He seemed to her a despicable, weak sort of character swayed by whoever he was with at the time. He had obviously returned to her influenced by his family — uneasy because he had contracted a secret marriage 'beneath him'. Such is the length and duration of passion without love. Phillip had wanted Cherry with a fierce passion and had married her because she had refused to surrender more than a kiss or two. He had had time to settle down . . . to get over that mad honeymoon in Paris . . . he was the typical male-creature, bored by what he could now call his 'own property'. Cherry was full of scorn. She despised men of his calibre. She thought of Bill's steady devotion . . . of how loyal he would be, all his life, to the girl he loved. To Bill love and respect were primary . . . passion only a secondary factor.

Cherry couldn't read her husband's thoughts, but she was sure she was right about his attitude toward her. Much later she learned how very right she had been — Phillip had met some particularly lovely and attractive Society girl when he had been home and he had asked himself why he had tied himself up to Cherry in such haste.

Cherry knew she had not greeted

him very charmingly; hadn't put herself out to be nice. She had sufficient confidence in her own attraction to believe that if she chose to fling herself into his arms and use all her wiles, she could bring Phillip to her feet again. He was very weak. But she didn't want to do that. Her one idea was to get away . . . to Bill.

It was now twenty-five minutes to eight. She was already five minutes late. She didn't want to keep Bill waiting too long. He might think her ill and come back to the flat . . . then the fat would be in the fire.

Phillip drew a thin gold case out of his pocket and lit the Turkish cigarette he pulled from it. He was scowling; thoroughly nettled.

'You're sulking,' he said. 'Really, Cherry, you are most exacting. I've only been away from you a week.'

Cherry ground her teeth. Fool — conceited ass — he thought she was annoyed because *he* had kept away from her. What did it matter? It was only his money she wanted. It was Bill, the man, who mattered to her.

'You've been very casual with me, anyhow,' she flashed. 'Not even phoning or writing.'

'I didn't have a moment to spare — honestly.'

'You've changed your tone. You're not quite the ardent lover you were,' Cherry said sneeringly.

He looked at her, still frowning. Then his brow cleared. He was struck suddenly by her slim unique beauty, standing there with her head flung back; cheeks flushed; hazel eyes large and brilliant with anger. In her plain tailored suit, she was lovely and she belonged to him. Passion for his possession stirred in him. He came up to her and put an arm about her.

'Don't let's fight, Cherry. I'm sorry if I appeared casual. But you're my wife and you know I'm absolutely clay in your hands. Cherry-ripe, I'll make up for it. We'll go out to dinner — where'd you like to go — The Savoy Grill — the

Caprice? Anywhere you like. Then we might go on to a show — have supper and dance at The Four Hundred.'

He mapped out a pleasant expensive evening. He caressed her cheek with a forefinger; pressed little affectionate kisses on her lips; grew fired by the touch; flung away his cigarette and tried to embrace her fiercely.

She stood speechless, unyielding, with black rage and contempt for him in her heart. She didn't want to go out with him. She wanted to keep her appointment with Bill. She clenched her hands . . . almost hysterical with worry. It was twenty-minutes to eight — ten minutes late. Bill might telephone. She felt she must act, do something to end her worry.

Cherry struggled out of her husband's arms. She faced him, panting, dishevelled, cheeks scarlet. She realised that the one and only thing she could do was to quarrel with him.

'I won't go out with you!' she stormed. 'I won't have you just turn up casually to suit yourself; expect me to be at your beck and call, ready to come out when you whistle for me. I won't be treated like . . . like your . . . *mistress*. It's bad enough that you can't acknowledge me to your people. But understand this; I'm not going to stand casual treatment, Phillip Bellairs . . . '

'Ssh,' he said, frowning and glancing at the door uneasily. 'Damn it, remember we are known as the *Gerards* . . . Anna might hear . . . '

'You think only of your reputation — not mine!' she broke in hysterically. (Part of it was genuine anger, part acting). 'I'm absolutely fed up. I've 'had it,' I won't stay another moment in this flat. I'm clearing out.'

He caught her arm, his face pale, slightly astonished to think that he had created this scene. He had never suspected his honey-sweet Cherry of having a temper.

'Darling, don't be silly. Darling — where are you going? Cherry!'

She ignored his appeal and shook off

his arm, dashed across the room, ran out and slammed the door in his face. The crash of it shook the flat. What he thought or imagined; where he supposed she was going, she didn't care. She only knew she must go to Bill; that no way else could she send a message and that he must be prevented from coming to the flat.

Phillip did not follow her. He was in a raging temper. The porter called a taxi for 'Madam' and Cherry told the driver to go to Oxford Circus Tube.

On the way there, Cherry's rage cooled. She felt altogether miserable and distressed at the turn events had taken. It was a disaster . . . Phillip's sudden arrival. The quarrel had been equally disastrous. She didn't really want Phil to dislike her . . . to stop her allowance and take a mean revenge. Later, when she got back she would have to play the seductive little wife . . . lure him back to her arms. But it was all hideously distasteful and her evening with Bill had been completely spoiled before it even started. How could she possibly enjoy it. She had bitten off more than she could chew.

She found Bill pacing up and down in the crowded street, anxiously awaiting her. She was twenty minutes late. And it had started to rain — a thin summer drizzle that made the streets look dismal and uninviting. Bill's suit was already damp, but he was as good-tempered as ever. So different from Phillip, she thought gloomily. Oh, how she wished that she belonged to Bill.

She explained that she had been delayed because 'Mr. Gerard' had returned. 'And I've got to go straight back,' she said, taking Bill's arm. 'Mrs. Gerard isn't going out now that her husband has come home. I've only dashed here to tell you I can't stay.'

Bill was bitterly disappointed. She wanted to weep herself. But she dared not keep away from her husband and her home, in case Phillip became suspicious. It was all very well for her to dash out of the flat in a temper, but she dared not stay out for long. There was no knowing what an angry thwarted Phillip might do. And after all, as far as he knew, Cherry was supposed to be in love with him; only just married; and not having a close friend in London.

Bill walked with her slowly down the street towards Piccadilly. They were unmindful of the drizzle. Arms pressed together, they walked like any other young couple whispering and talking.

'Awful shame, you must go back, darling. I'm so disappointed.'

'Me, too — terribly,' Cherry said, feeling tired and dejected. She stole a look at Bill's handsome profile and felt a sharp pain in her heart. He was so incredibly dear to her; so much dearer than Phillip could ever be in this world. If she lost him! Supposing he ever discovered what a bad mercenary character she had — a woman who wanted to eat her cake and have it — at any price! Or — if some other girl attracted him in Tunbridge Wells? She felt madly jealous at the mere thought of any other woman in Bill Carew's life.

She was altogether responsive, therefore, when Bill suddenly broached the subject of their marriage.

'Cherry, I shan't feel happy till you and I are married,' he said gloomily. 'I'd feel so much better if you belonged to me and I was leaving you, knowing that.'

'I feel that way, too, Bill darling,' she said.

He knit his straight brows.

'Cherry, I've a good mind to ask you to marry me at once.'

Her heart jerked.

'How could we?' she asked thickly.

'I'd have to dive into my few savings, such as they are, and get a special licence. If you could say some relative needed you for a few days and come to Tunbridge Wells, we might get married there. Then I could let you go more happily, knowing you were mine, Cherry.'

He spoke seriously. Cherry could see

he was dreading the parting from her; as jealous of leaving her as she was of leaving him . . . she was Phillip Bellair's wife. How could she do what she yearned to do . . . without committing *bigamy*. Ugh! Bigamy was an ugly word and against the law — a punishable crime. Yet with every drop of blood in her body she wanted to marry Bill . . . to belong to him . . . know he was bound to her.

Bill pressed her arm close to his side.

'Cherry,' he said eagerly. 'Would you do it? We'd have to keep it secret from Mr. Bellairs and the fellows who are training me. But it would be glorious — to know we are man and wife. Cherry, you love me . . . say 'yes' . . . say you'll come down to Tunbridge Wells next week and marry me.'

6

Cherry was quite stunned by Bill's intense and passionate outburst. It was wonderful; a frightful responsibility for her to have on her shoulders — the love (such love) of a man like Bill Carew.

'Cherry,' came his low, urgent voice. 'Cherry, my own — say that you will marry me.'

She felt faint and clung to his arm as they walked down the wet, shining pavements. The neon lights on the shops revolved in yellow circles before her eyes. She tried to collect her scattered thoughts. She knew, definitely, that she must give Bill an answer then or never. If she disappointed him he would leave her frustrated and disappointed. After all, so far as he knew, she had no ties. She was just a girl earning her living in a domestic job. She was madly in love with him. What reason would she have for refusing him? A secret marriage to any normal girl passionately in love would seem a thrilling thing — a huge temptation to which she would without doubt succumb. She was no different — could not resist the thrill and the temptation. What an utter fool she thought, to have married Phillip Bellairs. What did she care for her flat in 'American Square' as they called it; her aristocratic husband, her glamorous clothes? When she was actually in the midst of all the luxury she revelled in it. When she was out with Bill, Cherry wanted nothing, nobody but Bill.

Then she made up her mind to marry Bill Carew as he wanted — bigamy though it would be. She could not tolerate the idea of losing him. And she could not give Phillip up altogether. She was his wife. A divorce, even if Phillip agreed to one, would mean publicity; then Bill would know everything. *No, she must keep both.* She could be a wife to both and neither must ever know that the other existed. A dangerous game; a wicked one. But on that particular night when Bill pleaded with her she felt the desire to do as he asked — to bind herself to him forever.

Cherry looked up at his eager face and said:

'Yes, darling — very well — I *will* — I will marry you.'

His eyes flashed. He pressed her arm to his side.

'Oh, you angel, Cherry. My sweet, sweet Cherry. You are an absolute darling,' he said. 'I wish we were not in the street. Oh, Cherry, I do want to kiss you!'

His touch, his words were electric to her — shivering her — filling her with fresh intoxication. Or, if she were blind — she would still thrill hearing that caressing voice and see in her mind's eye the fascination of Bill's blue Irish eyes, with the short dark lashes.

'I want to kiss you, too,' she whispered.

He looked at her mouth. The very look was as a kiss of hot passion. She half-closed her eyes . . . clinging to his arm. As they walked along, she thought:

'I would do anything for this man — die for him — *I am going to commit bigamy for him!*'

She shivered not only with ecstasy of her love but with strange terror of what she meant to do. She was mad indeed, she, who had married Phillip Bellairs only a short while ago . . . to be contemplating another marriage . . . to take another husband!

Her mother would have died of horror . . . her nice, ordinary sisters, all her God-fearing relations . . . would be stricken and ashamed of the thing she meant to do. *Bigamy was a crime.* None of them would be capable of crime. What *was* it in her, Cherry Brown, that made her reckless and even criminal, she wondered? Yet even then a little wicked demon of pleasure rioted in her . . . pleasure and pride in herself and her own capabilities. It was a thrilling thing to hold men in the hollow of her hand as she held them; to have the power to inspire such passionate love, and return it.

Bill walked with Cherry back to the corner of her square. She let him come with her as far as that, but no further. She could not risk his running up against Phillip.

They had made their plans. Bill, on fire with enthusiasm because Cherry had agreed to the secret marriage, could scarcely restrain his excitement.

'It's too marvellous — to think that you will marry me. Why did we wait so long? We were a bit dumb, darling.'

'Yes, I know,' Cherry said. 'But even now we haven't got much money to marry on.'

'That's true — ' He hunched his shoulders. 'That's the worst part of it. You're so damned beautiful, Cherry, I want to buy you terrifically glamorous clothes and give you a home worthy of you. Instead . . . I can only marry you secretly and give you a bit of my savings. Phillip Bellairs is financing my training, but I don't make any money until I start to fight.'

'That's all right, darling,' Cherry said hastily. 'I don't want a cent.'

'All the same, I hate to think of you working for your living, Cherry. Once we are married, will you please leave this Mrs. Gerard and go back home . . . live quietly there. The idea of you working at any other woman's beck and call — '

'Rubbish, darling,' she interrupted quickly. 'I don't mind work and I couldn't bear to hang around at home doing nothing. Besides, you must hang on to your savings for our future.'

'One day I may be a rich man — middle-weight champion of Europe,' Bill said with a laugh.

'I'll wait till then,' Cherry said.

'You're sure you don't mind going on with your job for Mrs. Gerard?'

Cherry shook her head. She couldn't bear the thought of going home. She was quite attached to her mother and

Polly and all of them but she didn't want to lead that old dull life — and put up with a hard bed and badly cooked food and awful cheap clothes. Not while she could keep her new luxury and Anna to wait on her and every luxury Phillip's money could buy. These were the moments when the greedy Cherry asserted herself . . . the mercenary greedy Cherry. She adored Bill. But she wasn't going to give up everything that Phillip could give her — until Bill could afford to give her likewise. No! She needed them both for the moment — two loves. If she managed things cleverly she thought, she could keep everything. Bill's love; Phillip's money. She wanted Bill's love for love's sake . . . Phillip's for the sake of what he could give her. She was treading on the brink of a precipice . . . night and day. But she intended to go on trusting there would never be a fall.

Bill stopped at the corner of the Square; drew Cherry away from the lights into a shadowy entrance of a small hat shop, long since closed for the night. He took her hands and pressed the palms against his lips.

'Angel. I'll get the licence tomorrow. Will you give Mrs. Gerard some excuse to let you stay away from Saturday next till, say, Tuesday. Come down to Tunbridge Wells . . . I'll send you an address . . . and we'll be married in the local registry.'

Her heart beat madly. She looked up at him.

'You really think it wise?' She began weakly.

He just put his long, strong arms around her and crushed her mouth in a kiss that sent wisdom a long way from both of them. She did not make any further attempt to stem the burning tide that was carrying them both on to the high seas of passion and adventure. Cherry gave him her solemn promise to get away on Saturday for their marriage.

'If Mrs. Gerard kicks up rough, you

must just leave,' Bill added, holding her very close. 'But if you say it's a question of urgent personal affairs surely she'll be decent about it. It is going to be hell letting you go after only twenty-four hours of married life. I wonder if I can bear to let you go.'

Cherry swallowed hard. Her lips were dry. Her throat burned. The madness of it. To become Bill's wife, when already married to Phillip Bellairs. If Bill ever discovered the truth what would he think of Cherry? *What would he do to her?* She wondered if he would kill her first and himself afterwards.

'Don't tremble like that, angel,' she heard his voice against her ear. 'It'll be okay in time. You know I'll be good to you. I love every hair on your head. You're so sweet, so able. You aren't afraid of running away with your old Bill, are you?'

Scalding tears rushed to Cherry's eyes. He was so sweet, so full of adoration and respect. She felt base, mean, unworthy, yet in her queer, twisted way she loved him . . . she needed his love. Without him she felt that life would be empty and grey. She swung from passion to remorse, wishing that she'd never married Phillip . . . that she could go to Bill with a clean record . . . that she was all he believed her to be. She realised what a wrong she was going to do him . . . how grossly she would be deceiving him. He smiled, his eyes full of trust. It would have broken his honest heart if he could have read what lay in Cherry's mind.

She was as wax in his hands that night . . . passion-torn, crazy for him. She did not want to leave him immediately after their marriage, either. She intended to see this dreadful thing through; commit this sin, and she would do it thoroughly. She would stay with him on Saturday night, drink the cup of rapture to the brim before it was snatched from her. She would never be sure that one or the other of these men with whom she was playing, might not discover her guilt.

They kissed again and again . . . murmuring little broken words of passion in each other's arms. Then Cherry drew away from him.

'I must go, Bill. Good-night, darling.'

'Good-night, angel,' he said, 'I shall be on edge until Saturday.'

'So shall I,' Cherry whispered.

'I'll write,' he added. 'Good-night, Cherry.'

His voice echoed . . . *good-night* . . . as she ran from him; ran round the corner of the square into the big lighted flower-filled entrance of the small block of flats where she was known as *Mrs. Gerard*.

Bill went away quite happy. Cherry knew that. But the flush left her cheeks and the brilliance died from her eyes as she faced the front-door of her flat and queried what lay before her. Phillip might of course have gone out and stayed out in a temper. On the other hand he might be in there, waiting for

119

her. There would be a fierce row, reproaches, sulks, tears, reconciliation. It must be endured. She told herself grimly. Bill was still a poor man and she could not afford to lose Phillip's money — yet! But she dreaded the price she must pay for her financial security. With lips still throbbing from the pressure of Bill's lips, she had little desire for Phillip's caresses. He had never really appealed to her physically, and still less did he appeal since she became his wife.

Where there is only passion, familiarity breeds contempt. Cherry felt that there was a certain amount of contempt now between Phillip and herself. If desire was still in him — it had died in her. Nevertheless she had to keep on good terms with him.

Cherry let herself into the flat with her latch-key. She heard a clock strike the half-hour as she did so. Half-past nine — nearly two hours since she had rushed away to meet Bill.

She tip-toed to the drawing room

door and pushed it. Her pulses jerked as she saw Phillip sprawled on the sofa, smoking a cigar and reading an evening paper. He was still there, waiting for her. She took her courage in both hands and marched boldly into the room.

'Hello,' she said.

Philip let his paper fall to the floor and looked up at her with a cold, hostile expression.

'So you've deigned to come home,' he said.

She drew off her gloves; then took off her hat and ran her fingers through her thick chestnut curls. She decided to behave as though nothing had happened.

'Did Anna bring you a meal, Phillip?' she asked.

'No, I had it at the Club. I've only just come back.'

She threw him a casual glance and lit a cigarette.

'I've had nothing yet. I must get Anna to make me a sandwich if she has not gone home. Mrs. P. will be out. She asked if she could go out at nine sharp to see her daughter.'

Phillip rose and advanced towards her. Cherry stood quite still and he gripped her shoulders. He was white and his eyes were smouldering with resentment.

'Cherry, you've been out for over two hours. Where the hell have you been? *Who have you been with?*'

'Been with?' she repeated, simulating amazement. 'What do you mean, my dear Phillip?'

'Don't try and fool me,' he said. 'You went out of the flat at seven-thirty. You come home just before ten. Where have you been?'

'For a walk.'

'A damned long walk,' he sneered.

'Well, if you want the truth — I was furious with the way you've neglected me and I was in a foul temper,' she said. 'I admit it. I stayed out till my temper cooled. It is raining and I'm wet and cold and I'm going to pop into a hot bath if you don't mind.'

He glared down at her. The muscles of his cheeks were working. She thought he looked very unattractive, a slight, pale man with his spoiled mouth, his thin line of moustache, and angry eyes. How unlike Bill, her handsome healthy Bill with his bright blue eyes, his bronzed skin and magnificent figure. She saw Phillip's gaze rove over her suit and the little flowered cap on her head. It probably looked bedraggled and unattractive. But she had at least taken care to wipe the smudge of lip-stick from her mouth.

'You *are* wet,' he admitted. 'All the same, I'm not at all happy about you, Cherry. I have an instinctive feeling that you went out to meet another man, tonight.'

'Oh, don't be so ridiculous,' she snapped. 'I've had enough of men. I've married you and that's enough for me.'

He went on glaring at her, as though doubting her. But his grip on her shoulder slackened.

'Cherry, you swear you aren't playing

round with someone I don't know?'

'Of course, idiot!' she said impatiently. 'Since when have you become the jealous husband? It is for *me* to be jealous. You leave me alone for days. How do I know there isn't a woman somewhere keeping *you* from me?'

That was cunning. Phillip's hands fell to his sides. He looked mollified. He stroked his moustache.

'No, it was business — not a woman that kept me from you, Cherry,' he said. 'Look here, aren't we both making a mountain out of a molehill? We've both lost our tempers. Didn't I ask you to forget it and have an amusing evening before you rushed out in that state?'

'All right,' Cherry said. 'I'm quite willing to forget, if you are.'

Inwardly she chafed to get away from him; to stop this conversation. He irritated her. On the other hand she was rather pleased and gratified to find that he cared enough for her still to be jealous. He might regret that he had married her (having got her) but he didn't want any other man to have her, obviously.

She told herself that he hadn't really had a chance to grow sick of her, and that if she chose to make herself attractive to him she could still twist him round her little finger. She resolved to keep his affections. She wasn't going to lose him.

Before Phillip could say any more Cherry ran out of the room, telling him to uncork a bottle of champagne and to ring for sandwiches, while she got out of her day suit. Hastily she bathed, then put on one of her loveliest nightgowns — a most alluring mist of pale blue chiffon. Over this she slipped on the velvet dressing gown which Phillip admired; she brushed her hair into thick bright curls; rubbed a little rouge over her cheeks grown pale. A generous outlining of her wide sensuous lips with a new. lipstick — *Paint the Town Pink* it was called — and Cherry returned to the drawing-room. She was conscious that she looked her best; beautiful enough to stir any man. And her husband was a weak and easily-captured creature. He gave one look at her, then swung her into his arms. She felt his heart beating hard; saw half-shamed passion and even tenderness in his eyes — narrow, hard eyes after Bill's wide open blue ones.

'My Cherry-ripe, you *are* adorable. Damn it, I'm more than sorry for neglecting you. Darling, kiss me — you're an exquisite creature — born for love — it's incredible how my simple country girl has grown into a most sophisticated, glamorous woman.'

Cherry felt nothing but scorn for him, although she thrilled to find that she was still irresistible to Phillip. She let him carry her to the sofa and hold her tightly in his arms.

She felt sleepy. She wanted to close her eyes and think of Bill and her approaching marriage. Instead she had to play the part of seductress. It was maddening. Phillip kissed and caressed her and was so interested in what he personally had to say that he did not notice that Cherry did not respond to his caresses.

If any other girl had ever attracted him she was forgotten now. He was hotly in love with Cherry again. He kissed her until she felt she would scream and beat his face black.

'You're my wife, enchanting little Cherry-ripe,' he kept on saying, repeating his pet-name for her until she shivered with nerves and irritation.

She thought, 'No — my dear Phil, it's Bill I love and I am going to be his wife: I am going to give *him* kisses that you never get from me.'

Phillip's fingers burned through the filmy chiffon at her throat. He looked down at her with hot, passionate eyes, the other hand clasping the slim, tiny waist he so adored.

'Cherry, there's something about you that drives me crazy,' he said.

'Is there?' she asked lazily. She stroked his head mechanically, thinking how she would cover Bill's curly head with kisses . . . soon. Phillip said:

'I'll buy you the most super present I can afford tomorrow, Cherry. Would you like a pair of diamond clips?'

Diamonds always fascinated Cherry. Eagerly she accepted his offer and returned his caresses more sincerely.

'How sweet of you, Phil, darling. Thanks awfully!'

'I'll do more,' he said, kissing the nape of her neck.

'I'll take you over to France for the week-end. We'll go to Le Touquet, if you like.'

Cherry's heart leaped at that. *Le Touquet* . . . Paris Plage — the Casino . . . one of the most fashionable in Europe. But for the week-end, no! Impossible. On Saturday she had to be in Tunbridge Wells. She said:

'Next week it would be thrilling, Phillip. But on Saturday I — I have to run down to Dalescombe and see mother. I had a card from Polly yesterday. Mum has been very seedy. I don't want to disappoint her.'

'You shall do just what you want, my adorable,' he said. He was in the best of humours now. And Cherry's heart gave a great throb of relief. Thank goodness! *That* danger was over. They arranged that they would remain in the flat together till the week-end. Then she (presumably) would go to Dalescombe and return to the flat the following Tuesday. They would then fly to Le Touquet.

Everything seemed all right. The way appeared clear and the prospect rosy. She slept soundly in Phillip's arms that night. But in her dreams there was no Phillip. It was Bill, her first love, who held her to his heart.

7

Saturday morning.

Cherry's wedding-day. It seemed to her utterly wild and impossible when she woke up and remembered the fact. Her second wedding-day within a few weeks. Yet it was immensely thrilling. But she had to admit to herself that from the second she woke up she was uneasy and afraid. She felt that she must go on with what she had set out to do. But she was frightened because of the crime she meant to commit. In another 24 hours *she would be a bigamist*.

Phillip offered to drive her down to Dalescombe. Cherry got out of that difficulty by telling him that her sister Polly was coming up to town to meet her and do some shopping and that they were travelling down by train together. Phillip never suspected any wrong and let her go without further question. She had been charming to him since their quarrel and he was thoroughly enamoured of her again. He was going to stay with his own people that week-end he said, but he would only live for the moment when she was in his arms again.

She left him feeling that she never wanted to see him again. Her whole mind was concentrated on Bill. In her purse lay a letter from Bill with full instructions. He had obtained the special licence and she was to meet him at midday at the registry office in Tunbridge Wells. She had wired him. 'Got leave to stay three days. All love, Cherry.'

Two whole days and nights of ecstasy stretched before her. Of perfect happiness as Bill's wife. But all the way to Tunbridge Wells, alone in the train, her conscience troubled her. She felt cold and nervous. She was doing such a terrible thing. Would she get through with what she meant to do? Would she?

Alternately she thrilled with the excitement and reproached herself for the wrong she was about to do Bill. She even hated herself for the wrong she was doing to Phillip.

But she went on . . . the moth blindly circling round the flame . . . scorching her wings — yet impelled by an unknown force to dash herself nearer and nearer to total destruction.

Cherry tried to assure herself that she was clever enough to win the day; to keep both the men she wanted. She tried to deafen her ears to the voice of her conscience; to submerge all that was good and decent in her. By the time she reached Tunbridge Wells she was mistress of herself — cool and calm and prepared to throw herself recklessly into the spirit of the day. The Day of days . . .

It was a lovely morning; one of those soft, gold days of late September when the warmth of the sun breaks through the autumn mists. The historic old town was looking its best. Cherry, who had never seen it before, loved it. Bill's future training centre. The place where she was to spend the two wild, mad days of her honeymoon with Bill. The trees were gold and russet-red. The flower shop windows were gay with the bronze and gold and purple of autumn flowers. The very breath of romance seemed to fan her cheeks when finally she stepped out of the train and gave her hand to Bill, who was on the platform waiting for her. They drove straight to the registry office.

Cherry felt only one qualm . . . and that was when Bill slipped a gold wedding-ring on her finger and the Registrar pronounced them man and wife. It was a terribly serious moment for her. Her heartbeats shook her slim body. She felt sick and faint as she contemplated the gravity of it. She was Cherry Bellairs — not Cherry Carew. She set her teeth when she realised how little that gold ring of Bill's meant . . . for it was not the first that had been placed there.

But Bill, unconscious of her agonising reflections was like a great boy, bubbling over with good spirits and happiness. He kissed her tenderly before they left the room in which that brief ceremony had been performed, with two strangers as witnesses.

'My wife,' he whispered. 'Oh, Cherry — mine at last!'

She kissed him back and Cherry wished that she were indeed his wife and that the past could be wiped out.

Bill took a taxi from the registry office.

'I'm going to be extravagant to-day,' he said. 'A man only has one wedding day. We'll drive to the Bridge Hotel. The grounds are so beautiful and it's a luxury hotel and for our one or two nights, darling . . . why not?'

Cherry thrilled to his voice: to the passion in his eyes.

'Yes, why not, my dear?' she asked. But she felt miserable when she thought over his words: 'A man only has one wedding-day.' This was her second one

. . . within a few short weeks.

Desperately she strove to put the remembrance of that other marriage; that other husband, from her mind. She looked at Bill's brown face; the perfect health and strength and grace of him.

Cherry left her suitcase at the station. They drove there to pick it up on their way to the hotel.

In the taxi Bill crushed her against him. She felt his lips — like fire on her mouth. The spray of white carnations he had pinned to her coat were bruised.

'Two days, two nights, darling, let us make these hours the most wonderful of our lives,' he said. 'Later, when my training is over and I can claim you, it will still be wonderful. But to-night will be unrepeatable. Let us love each other with all our hearts, all our minds, all our souls . . . '

Cherry clung to him, fired by his passion. There was something so much finer and cleaner and deeper in Bill's love than Phillip's, and it affected

Cherry accordingly.

'Yes, with all our hearts and minds and souls, Bill,' she echoed. Then added, half despairingly: 'Oh, my darling, whatever happens in the future, remember that we loved each other like this.'

'You bet I will,' he said with a ringing laugh and kissed the ring he had just put on her finger. (Phillip's was in a case in a drawer in her London flat.)

Almost she forgot the broken law — the shame of her action in that hour. They kept the taxi waiting while they went into the station to collect Cherry's suitcase. They could not bear to be separated for a single moment. Cherry flung herself into the present and walked on air . . . daring to visualise the ecstasy ahead of her.

Then the catastrophe happened . . . the unbelievable and terrible thing.

As they walked out of the station into the warm, soft air, Bill suddenly dropped her case and gave a cry.

'Look! Look, Cherry!'

She looked . . . her heart leapt to her throat. She saw a small child; a girl of three or four, toddling onto the road after a ball. She saw a lorry bearing down upon her. Before she realised what was happening, Bill had sprung forward and clutched the child's arm and flung her behind him into safety. The lorry pulled up with a grinding of brakes. But not before the right mud-guard had caught Bill and thrown him. Cherry saw him go down in the dust, before her horrified eyes; saw the right wheel of that great, cruel lorry hit him, pinning him where he had fallen. He lay still, his splendid body motionless . . . his face hidden on an arm which he had flung across it as though to save his eyes.

Cherry thought she would die of shock. She rushed forward and threw herself down on the road beside him. She took his head on her lap and cried his name aloud in an agony of fear.

'Bill! Bill! . . . oh, Bill, are you dead?

Bill, open your eyes — speak to me — for the love of God — speak to me, Bill!'

8

Cherry almost fainted as she sat there in the road with Bill's head on her lap, frantically calling his name and imploring him to speak to her. His face was not touched; only bruised and soiled. She pulled out a handkerchief to wipe the dust from his cheek; the trickle of blood from a scratch on his chin. But his eyes were closed and his lips pale and sucked in. He did not answer her cries.

The morbid crowd hustled up and gathered round. It was astonishing where all the people came from. Bill and Cherry were surrounded. They were under the black shadow of the great lorry which had pulled up sharply. But one of the monster wheels had caught Bill on the left shoulder. (How utterly thankful Cherry was for his sake when she heard, later, that his right arm was untouched . . . that strong, long arm which was to deal the knock-out blow to an opponent in the ring in the days to come!)

There was utter confusion . . . people . . . vehicles . . . traffic held up . . . cries . . . exclamations of pity and horror . . . and then the burly form of a policeman, then two more of them pushing back the crowd. Cherry heard one say:

'Keep back, keep back there — give 'im air . . . '

Somebody touched her shoulder.

She dragged herself back to full consciousness of the terrible accident. Through a kind of mist, she saw a policeman's kindly face.

'Gentleman your 'usband, mam?'

She had to bite her lower lip to keep herself from saying:

'Yes, yes, he is mine . . . mine . . . '

But she stopped in time. She had just sufficient sense left to remember that if she publicly described herself as Mrs. Carew, it would get into the papers . . . she might be photographed

. . . heaven knows what. She dared not say that she was his wife. So she just gasped:

'No — my — my friend.'

The policeman took the elastic band off his notebook and with legs planted apart and pencil poised began to question her in his formal, stilted fashion.

'The gentleman's name, please, miss.'

She answered his enquiries . . . giving Bill's address in Tunbridge Wells. She had just come down from London, she said, to spend the day with her friend. The luggage? Her cheeks grew hot and her brain confused as he pointed over his shoulder to the suitcase which had been dropped when Bill rushed to rescue the child.

She said:

'Oh, the cases are mine. I — I was going to take rooms down here for a bit.'

Then an ambulance arrived. Stretcher-bearers took Bill away from Cherry — lifted him from the ground — put him on a stretcher — gently — very gently. But as they moved him he opened his eyes and moaned. That moan of pain nearly broke Cherry's heart. She burst into wild weeping.

'Bill . . . Bill . . . '

The constable touched her on the shoulder.

'It's all right, miss. He isn't dead by a long chalk. The ambulance nurse thinks it's only a broken collarbone and a few nasty bruises and cuts. Bit of concussion — shock you know.'

Only that! But to Cherry it was a dire catastrophe. This was the end of her honeymoon. There would be no golden hours of passionate love, of love's laughter. Only a casualty ward in a hospital for her Bill and loneliness, unbearable, and torturing for her . . . she could scarcely contain herself. She hid her face in her hands and sobbed, bitterly.

A woman put an arm around her. Cherry looked up at her through scalding tears. She, too, was crying. She was the mother of the child whom Bill had saved.

'He was a hero, God bless him. He saved my little girl from death. You should be proud of him. He'll get the George Cross for this!'

Cherry was proud of him. How could she help it? How could she help being glad he had saved a child's innocent life?

Yet deep down in her burned deepest resentment against the ironic Fate which had thus shaped their Destiny. To have the cup of rapture snatched from her very lips ... Bill to be stricken down in the prime of his strength. She robbed of her love, just when things had seemed perfect, when life was glorious and the immediate future had held promise of indescribable happiness.

She supposed that this was a visitation upon her for her sins ... a punishment for the deception she had practised on two men for her own selfish ends.

Cherry was told she could go to the hospital with Bill and hear exactly the extent of his injuries. She decided to act with caution. She had to remember that although nobody in the world except Bill knew that she had come down to marry him, and everything had appeared to work out very nicely, she must be extremely careful. She was Phillip Bellairs' wife. Phillip expected her back in Connor Court on Tuesday. He imagined she was at home. She must act warily; no matter how heartbroken she was with disappointment; no matter how frantically worried about Bill.

Cherry decided to put their suitcases back in the station luggage office. That would ensure their safety. She dared not risk anyone opening them and discovering both Bill's clothes and hers — evidence that they had intended to spend a night together.

Cherry took a taxi to the hospital, following the ambulance. Her face was pale, streaked with tears as she sat in the waiting room for what seemed an interminable time. She pictured vividly what was happening. She harrowed herself with visions of Bill in the operating theatre, being examined . . . that poor, crushed collarbone set — bandaged . . . and perhaps worse injuries would be discovered . . . terrible, internal injuries. Perhaps Bill was dying. Perhaps he was already dead; she would never again see those Irish eyes smiling down at her; never again hear that husky voice saying:

'Cherry, my sweet Cherry!'

She was a miserable bundle of nerves when at length a white-gowned nurse in uniform came softly into the room to her. The nurse looked at her kindly.

'You are Miss Brown?'

'Yes,' Cherry said. (She had given her name as Miss Brown.) 'Tell me quickly. Is he . . . ?'

'He is going on nicely,' the nurse said. A frightful load of despair and doubt was taken off Cherry's shoulders. 'As well as can be expected. But it was

145

a nasty accident. I hear he was quite a hero — saving a child's life — '

'Yes,' Cherry said, chokingly. 'He is wonderful.'

'And you are his girlfriend?' she asked kindly.

'Yes,' Cherry replied sullenly. She hated having to say she was only Bill's 'girlfriend'; to hide her wedding ring under her glove. She wanted to blazon it abroad that she was Bill's wife. She fully expected the first name Bill would call on was 'Cherry'. But he would not say 'My wife'. He had his own reasons for not wishing to publish the fact that he was married. His reputation as a professional boxer was at stake. He had promised his manager, his trainer, that he would remain unmarried. He had told Phillip (his promoter) that he was a single man.

They would, doubtless, all come to see him in the hospital. He would send word to the trainer with whom he lived. He must not give away the fact that he was married.

Cherry wondered, with a sick feeling in her heart, what would happen if Bill decided to throw up his career as a boxer after this accident, and tell everybody that he had married her. Then, indeed, the fat would be in the fire. She would never be able to continue her dangerous game; keep her two husbands from discovering the truth.

Then Cherry heard the nurse telling her something which was totally unexpected and startling.

'You must prepare yourself for rather bad news, Miss Brown. Mr. Carew is going on well, in one way, but you know he had a blow on his head as well as injuries to his collar-bone. At the moment he has concussion.'

'Concussion!' Cherry echoed. 'You mean he is — unconscious?'

'Yes. Quite.'

'I can't see him. He wouldn't know me?'

'I'm afraid he wouldn't.'

Cherry's heart began to pound. Her

cheeks grew fiery.

'You are trying to tell me he is very bad!'

'No, no, my dear,' said the nurse gently. 'Don't upset yourself too much. He is not going to die. But that lorry caught his head and that is what is worrying the doctors most. The collar-bone is a minor injury, and he has a magnificent constitution and is in perfect health. He'll mend rapidly enough. But one never quite knows what will happen to the memory after severe concussion.'

'Oh — my God — his memory — he might lose it — forget everything and everybody!'

'I hope not, but it is best for you to be prepared,' the nurse said. 'If you will give me your name and address I will keep you informed — let you know as soon as he recovers consciousness.'

Cherry's head seemed to be going round. She could scarcely think. If that blow to the head had injured Bill's brain, how much more of a tragedy that would be than any injury to his body. She stumbled to a chair. The nurse stood talking, to her in a soothing voice.

'Everything will be all right in time — don't lose hope,' she said. 'By the way, has he any relations we should inform?'

Cherry thought of Bill's old mother in Little Cross. She ought to be told, of course. She gave her name and address mechanically. But she thought:

'She must not know about Miss Brown, otherwise she will guess it's me. The news will spread all over Dalescombe. Then Phillip will hear.'

She decided to concoct a story. Hurriedly she told the nurse that her engagement to Bill was secret, and asked that when his mother arrived at the hospital she should not be told about 'the girlfriend.'

'You're human, I'm sure, nurse,' Cherry said, clutching her hand. 'You understand these things. You won't give me away — or let the other nurses do so.'

The nurse promised to keep their secret. She was certainly human; had understanding and sympathy for lovers in difficulties. She promised to say nothing about Cherry to Mrs. Carew.

Cherry then gave her the name and address of Bill's manager.

'Mr. Carew is a boxer and he was training for a big fight,' Cherry said huskily. 'Oh, what a catastrophe it all is.'

'Cheer up — he'll live to box again,' said the nurse. 'I'm 'specialised' to look after him for a day or two and I promise to do my utmost for him and to keep you informed as to his condition.'

For the first time Cherry's brain grew clear and she looked at the nurse, not as a machine of the hospital, but as a woman, who was to be Bill's special nurse. As Cherry stared at her, a vague sensation of uneasiness crept over her. This nurse was altogether too young and too good-looking. More than that. She was quite beautiful; tall, slender, with well-shaped hands and a face that might have belonged to an Italian

Madonna. A perfect oval; with pale olive skin and grave red lips. She had none of Cherry's vitality — her exciting big mouth and dancing eyes. But she was most attractive, and her eyes were lovely, very dark, and her hair — what was visible under her cap, a rich auburn. She certainly looked as though she came from Italy or Spain.

She was a year or two older than Cherry. But there was an air of graceful youth about her, which combined with the wisdom of almond-shaped eyes and sweet lips, produced a very charming result. Cherry could see at a glance that this girl was all that she was not; had all the virtues she lacked. Truth and candour shone from those dark eyes. She was a hospital nurse — dedicated — unselfish — the antithesis of naughty Cherry.

All this struck Cherry like a blow. She felt little and mean and her beauty, although fresher and more brilliant than the nurse's, seemed suddenly tarnished. Jealousy seized Cherry and tormented her at the idea that this charming nurse was to be Bill's 'special'; that she would sit at his bedside; that her capable fingers would minister to his needs; her wise brown eyes watch for his returning consciousness. Possibly her face would be the first he would see when he became conscious.

A look of dark envy clouded Cherry's face. The young nurse stared at her worriedly and said suddenly:

'Is anything wrong? Do you feel ill?'

'No,' Cherry almost snapped. 'I'm all right. I'm going now. If you want me overnight, please communicate with me at the Station Hotel. I shall be staying there. I'll come early tomorrow to see Mr. Carew. Phone for me if you need me tonight.'

Cherry's abrupt tone and queer expression upset the nurse. She flushed and said in a voice as cold as Cherry's:

'Very well, Miss Brown. I will remember your address.'

Cherry stared at her darkly. How

proud, how authoritative this nurse was. What a lot of excellent qualities she had. Cherry felt that if this girl knew how basely she had acted she would turn from her in scorn. Janet Barnes would not have stooped to commit crimes for the sake of personal gain.

Then Cherry felt a fool for allowing the beauty and personality of a strange girl on the nursing staff distress her. Why should she be jealous? Bill adored *her*. He would never look twice at his nurse. She was unstrung; her emotions distorted after the shock of the accident. She realised she must control herself. And it would be silly of her to make an enemy of Bill's 'special' nurse. Cherry walked up to her and held out both her hands.

'Oh, Sister, I'm simply off my head with worry,' she said brokenly.

She knew that when she spoke and acted like that, no man or woman ever resisted her. There were tears in those eyes which were so lustrous and beautiful under their curving lashes; her lips quivered childishly; she looked a pathetic, unhappy young woman. And Sister Janet Barnes immediately took Cherry's fingers in hers, squeezed them hard and was as nice and understanding as before.

'You poor dear. Of course you must be terribly upset, but cheer up,' she said. 'I'll take care of your young man.'

'Tell me your name,' said Cherry.

'Jan Barnes. Jan — short for Janet,' she said and smiled as though they were firm friends.

But when Cherry left the hospital she felt that she hated 'Jan'. She would sit by Bill while Cherry would be all alone in the dreary Station Hotel, waiting news of him. Why she felt so insanely jealous of Nurse Barnes, Cherry could not explain. She was a stranger to Bill; he was only a patient . . . One of hundreds to her . . . she would mean nothing to him. Cherry consoled herself with these and many other thoughts. Yet all that night she was haunted by the beauty of that dark-eyed girl and the dread that Bill would be attracted to her. Those who believe in premonition will understand this ... for assuredly Cherry must have sensed the fact, in the very beginning, that Nurse Barnes was to play a very important part in both Bill's life — and hers.

9

The night following Bill's accident Cherry felt miserable and tormented. If ever a woman suffered for her sins, Cherry had her share of suffering all through those long, lonely hours in the Station Hotel.

Only that morning she had been bubbling over with high spirits; glowing with ardour; with enthusiasm for life and love.

And now — darkness and desolation; the ashes of bitter disappointment.

In a small, cheap bedroom in the hotel Cherry sat most of the night, unable to go to bed and sleep; staring out of the window at the roof-tops and station goods yard — the dreary vista from her back room.

She had choked down a few mouthfuls of supper. But she was not hungry. She felt sick and wretched. She hated this miserable little bedroom; hated being alone. She could think of nothing but Bill lying on his narrow bed in the casualty ward of the hospital. Would he recover consciousness? Would he ask for her? Would sister Barnes send for her if he did ask? Were the injuries to his brain very severe? *Would he know her and remember everything that had taken place, when he did awaken?*

A hundred doubts and fears assailed Cherry.

The fact that it was a mild, starlit night mocked her misery. She looked up at those glittering stars and ground her teeth. The cruelty of Fate! By rights, at this hour, she should have been with her husband; in a big, beautiful bedroom; the bridal suite to which Bill would have taken her. She should have been in his arms — crushed to his heart — treading the path of rapturous reality instead of descending alone into the depths of her broken dreams. She should have found perfect passion and contentment which she could only find in Bill's arms. She could forget the sin and danger; lulled by the narcotic of his caresses.

Cherry cried until her eyes were red and her face swollen and distorted. But she did not care. She finally flung herself fully dressed on the bed and dug her nails into the pillow; sobbing frenziedly for Bill. It was dawn before she fell into the sleep of mental and physical exhaustion.

She awoke to a new sense of anxiety. Sunday . . . church bells ringing . . . the sun shining . . . a perfect September day again. As she washed and dressed, her heart was heavy. She looked white and devastated by her passionate despair of the previous night. Her eyes were circled with violet shadows. Her only desire was to get to the hospital and hear news of Bill.

Cherry felt distracted by the knowledge that soon she would have to return to Phillip and accompany him to Le Touquet. She could scarcely bear the prospect of leaving England . . . her darling Bill when he was dangerously ill in hospital . . . in need of her. He would think she did not love him if she was not at his side when he needed her. Yet she had to satisfy Phillip's demands or ruin everything.

Sister Barnes came to Cherry in the waiting-room, that Sunday morning. She saw at a glance that there wasn't any news. She said regretfully:

'I'm afraid Mr. Carew is still unconscious.'

Cherry put a hand to her head. It ached horribly and the bright sunshine streaming through the windows into the bare room with its glossy wooden floor and horrible odour of antiseptics, hurt her eyes. She felt consumed by grief.

'What shall I do?' she moaned, half to herself.

Sister Barnes put a hand on Cherry's shoulder.

'Would you like to see him, my dear? Of course he is still unconscious and it might distress you.'

Cherry shuddered.

'Yes, it's no use seeing him. What do the doctors say?'

'They know no more at present than last night. It is just a case of severe concussion. All the cuts and bruises will heal beautifully and his collar-bone is set. Once we get that head right he will soon be all right.'

Cherry thought, with despair, of Phillip, and their forthcoming trip to France. How could she leave Bill! She said:

'Have . . . any other people come to inquire after him yet?'

'His mother telegraphed to say she would be up during this afternoon with his uncle, from a place called Little Cross.'

'Yes,' Cherry said, dully. 'And anybody else?'

'A Mr. Frinton, who I understand is his manager, telephoned last night after you'd gone to express his distress and regret and to say that he and Mr. Wilson, his trainer, would be coming to inquire at the hospital some time today and would bring round some of his things.'

Cherry nervously received this news. She must leave the hospital before Mr. Frinton and Joe Wilson turned up. Sister Barnes had promised to send a note round to the hotel if there were any further news of Bill. As she was on duty till 6 p.m. she would arrange with one of the nurses off duty to deliver it.

Cherry wandered round Tunbridge Wells for the rest of that morning; miserable; dejected; waiting for Sister Barnes' note. She felt a wreck and looked it. She told herself she must try and eat and pull herself together, otherwise when Phillip saw her he would wonder what was wrong.

She struggled through the midday dinner at the hotel. A typically British meal; roast beef; cabbage; boiled potatoes; apple-tart and custard; cheese. She hated the dull people round her; commerical travellers; a couple of noisy old women; farmers having a meal out; noisily discussing their crops. There was no comfort, no distraction to be got out of such a place for Cherry. But she had no option but to stay there. It was the cheapest hotel in the district and she hadn't much money on her.

Then came a note from Sister Barnes. Cherry devoured it eagerly.

'Dear Miss Brown (she wrote),

I regret to tell you there is very little change in Mr. Carew's condition. His mother arrived and was very distressed. She saw him, but of course he did not know her. His uncle has also been here and has taken Mrs. Carew back to Little Cross. Mr. Frinton and Mr. Wilson called for news.

Come again tomorrow and let us hope for better things. I will do all I can to help you.'

Yours sincerely,
Jan Barnes.'

Cherry brooded over the letter and

realised how kind Jan Barnes had been to write; to promise to help her, in the belief that Bill and she were secretly engaged. Yet Cherry could not stifle the strange feeling of jealousy. Sister Barnes . . . Janet . . . with the beautiful face and eyes of velvet brown.

Two more dreadful torturing nights passed. Cherry thought she would go mad. And when Tuesday morning dawned she was faced with the most agonising problem. Phillip expected her back in town. Bill would expect her to remain in Tunbridge Wells. She did not know what to do.

The last three days shook her badly. She looked weak and ill. She took a taxi to the hospital because the rain poured down from a leaden sky and she had no umbrella. She waited miserably for Bill's nurse. She felt if Bill did not recover consciousness soon he would die . . . then everything would be ended . . . and she would want to die too.

Sister Barnes came into the room.

'My dear, he has opened his eyes and

spoken at last,' she said, her dark eyes shining. 'He came back to consciousness a short while ago.'

'Oh, thank God, thank God!' Cherry said hysterically.

'But wait,' Sister Barnes added. 'I'm afraid there is fresh trouble for you. He is sensible now, but what the doctors feared has come about. That blow has affected his memory.'

Cherry stared aghast.

'You mean he has lost it completely?'

'Yes, he can remember nothing that happened before the accident. He did not even remember his own name. When I told him I tried to jog his memory, he accepted what I said but he could not verify it in his own mind.'

The blood rushed to Cherry's temples. Her throat felt hot and dry. She clutched Sister Barnes' arm.

'Take me to him,' she said. 'Take me quickly. He loves me. When he sees me he will know me. Oh, he must . . . he shall . . . take me to him at once!'

10

Sister Janet Barnes put her arms around Cherry.

'You must control yourself before I can let you into the ward,' she said in a firm though gentle voice. 'Remember, Mr. Carew is a sick man. I can't have him upset by any display of emotion from a visitor!'

Cherry tried to curb her hysteria. She bit her lower lip till the blood came. She hated this self-possessed, calm young nurse; hated her authoritative voice and manner! She was annoyed that Janet Barnes could feel such concern for Bill — she who was a stranger to him.

But Cherry saw the necessity for control. She buried her face in her hands, laboured for breath; checked furious tears.

Janet Barnes said very gently:

'Don't lose heart. He may know you when he sees you.'

Cherry flung her head back, as she felt more composed. She swallowed hard and clenched her hands. She wanted Bill to recognise her. It was to her intolerable that the man she loved more than anything or anybody in the world should not know her.

'Take me to him, please, Sister,' she said.

They moved toward the door. But before Sister Barnes could open it, it was opened from the other side and a probationer thrust in her head.

'Two visitors for Mr. Carew, please, Sister.'

'Oh, dear, what a nuisance,' Sister Barnes murmured.

Cherry went cold with fear. *Who were the visitors?* It was essential to her that she should not be seen by anybody who knew Phillip, her real husband.

Sister Barnes glanced at Cherry.

'I know you want your visits kept secret,' she whispered. 'But I'm afraid I can't stop nurse from showing these people in here.'

Cherry asked: 'Can't we slip into the ward quickly before they come — ?'

Then she stopped and her heart seemed, to burst. Hot colour rushed to her cheeks; then receded. Two men had walked into the little waiting-room. One she recognised from a snapshot which Bill had shown her one day. Harry Frinton, the boxing manager. And the other . . . immaculately dressed, smart, with a rather bored look on his face . . . was *her husband, Phillip Bellairs*.

Cherry wished the ground would open up and swallow her. She felt absolutely terrified; like a trapped rabbit. Her knees wobbled. Sister Barnes' quick dark eyes noticed the sickly pallor of Cherry's face, and held her arm tightly. She knew that Cherry did not wish to disclose the real reason for visiting Bill and maintained a discreet silence for which Cherry was most thankful. If one tactless word was said the fact that Cherry had been in

Tunbridge Wells that night . . . the fat would indeed have been in the fire.

Cherry hoped that she would be able to avert the disaster which threatened her.

She nerved herself to face Phillip. His thin, sallow face went red with sheer amazement: his eyes, ludicrously round and astonished, stared at her. He came forward and without pausing to wonder whether he was behaving with discretion or otherwise, he exclaimed:

'Cherry! You here?'

She tried to smile.

'I'm equally surprised to see you,' she answered.

The expression of astonishment changed to one of cold displeasure.

'Why are you here?' he asked abruptly.

Cherry's heart pounded. She felt a kind of singing in her ears as she tried, desperately, to appear unconcerned.

'I — heard from Mrs. Carew that her son had had this accident and I — I came to inquire after him for *her*,' she said on the spur of the moment.

Sister Barnes' eyebrows shot up in amazement at Cherry's lie. She was fast coming to the conclusion that there was something 'fishy' about this affair, but she made no comment. With a tact which seemed inborn, she suddenly turned to Harry Frinton and said:

'Mr. Carew is a bit better since you last came. But I don't want him to have too many visitors at once. Would you care to come through and see him before this other gentleman and — er — young lady?'

'Oh, thanks,' said Frinton. He glanced at Phillip. 'Shall I do that, sir?'

'Yes, do,' said Phillip. 'I'll come along later.'

'I hope he will recognise you, Mr. Frinton,' said Sister Barnes. 'You know, it's so sad, his memory has completely gone.'

'You don't say, nurse! Poor fellow . . . ' Their voices died away.

Cherry found herself alone with her husband.

She realised that she must lie now, and lie desperately, unless she wanted to let the cat right out of the bag. She always had a quick, scheming brain and it served her well as she calmly addressed Phillip.

'You needn't look so surprised, my dear Phillip. Naturally I came along when Mrs. Carew asked me to. You know I'm staying the week-end with mother. Well, our family has been friends with the Carews for years. Mrs. Carew has no money to speak of and I could afford the fare here so I came along.'

'I see,' said Phillip, but his manner suggested that he did not 'see' at all and that he half suspected a mystery. He added: 'When I first met you, Cherry, I believe you were carrying on a kind of affair with this fellow. Are you sure your interest in him is purely on account of his mother?'

Cherry wanted to scream. She yearned to say:

'*No — I love Bill — adore him. I hate you!*'

But instead, she said:

'My dear, why all this fuss? You know perfectly well I have no real interest in Bill Carew except for old friendship's sake. I've come on his mother's behalf. It bored me to tears — all the way from Dalescombe to Tunbridge Wells on a Sunday morning. A foul journey.'

She spoke so casually that it must have impressed Phillip that she was being quite frank and open with him. The look of jealousy and distrust in his narrow eyes vanished. He took her hands; leaned down and kissed her on the lips.

'Darling — sorry for being so silly,' he said contritely. 'I was jealous for the moment. I knew Carew used to be in love with you?'

'Well, I was never in love with him,' Cherry said and inwardly asked heaven to forgive her *that* lie, above all others!

'And so you heard about this poor chap's accident?'

'Yes, Mrs. Carew sent over to

Dalescombe last night with the message,' she replied.

'It's a rotten affair,' he said dropping her hands and pulling the now familiar gold cigarette case from his pocket.

Cherry told herself, with a sudden leap of heart, that she was not supposed to know about Phillip's interest in Bill. She had averted her own personal danger. She was relieved beyond all words about that. But she had to play the game to the finish.

'What are you doing here, showing all this concern about Bill Carew?' she demanded. 'Who was that man who came with you?'

'He is Bill's manager.'

'Manager?' she inquired innocently.

'Surely you have heard in Dalescombe that Bill Carew is training to be a champion boxer?'

'I heard rumours, yes. So that is his manager? Then what are you?'

'I'm the promoter. I have put up the money.'

'Why didn't you tell me before?'

172

'My dear girl, a man doesn't tell his wife all his private business. Financing Carew for middle-weight champion was my little side-line — a kind of amusement. I'm very keen about boxing.'

'I see,' Cherry said rather bitterly. 'You love me so much you just don't tell me any of your affairs.'

Phillip took her hand and stroked it. His face became good-humoured.

'There, there, don't be sulky, Cherry. We had a wonderful night together on Friday. I fell in love with you all over again. Don't let's break the spell. We're off to France for our second honeymoon tomorrow, you know, darling. You need a holiday. You're looking paler and more shadowy-eyed than I've ever seen you. Not ill, are you?'

'No, no — nothing wrong — just a slight bilious attack yesterday,' she muttered.

She wanted to snatch her hand from him. The mere notion of a 'second honeymoon' in France with Phillip drove her frantic. She could not leave Bill when he would need her to help him get well. She wished she could send Phillip away and stay with Bill.

She wondered, ironically, what Phillip would say if he knew that his protege had been just about to start off on a honeymoon with her — when he was knocked down by that lorry.

Before Cherry could speak to Phillip again, there were footsteps and voices outside the door. Phillip dropped her hand.

'I mustn't let Frinton know we're married,' he whispered. 'Remember it's a dead secret to my family, still. Just let Frinton think we're friends.'

'All right,' Cherry replied, but she was not certain that she was out of the wood. She had not seen Bill yet. If she were forced to see him with Phillip and he recognised her . . . what then?

Sister Barnes and Mr. Frinton walked into the room.

Frinton — a big, stout man with a reddish face and bald head — was mopping his brow.

'Bless my soul, that was the most trying moment of my life, sir,' he said, addressing Phillip. 'The poor chap has lost his memory completely. Doesn't even remember who he is or what he was doing. Didn't know me from Adam! I doubt he'll ever put on the gloves again, sir — unless he recovers.'

Cherry felt sick with misery. Her poor Bill, his mind was a complete blank.

Phillip said:

'How very unfortunate, Frinton — when he promised so well.'

'He was a wonder, sir; would have beaten any champion living by the end of the year,' said Frinton.

'I'll go and say a few words to the poor chap,' said Phillip. He turned to Cherry: 'Will you come too?' he asked with formal courtesy.

'I — perhaps he ought not to see two visitors at once,' she muttered.

Sister Barnes, who had been tactful previously, forgot Cherry's delicate position and hastily said:

'Oh, that's all right. You can go in with him, Miss Brown.'

Cherry could have killed her. Phillip immediately said:

'Come along, then.'

She had no choice but to go. She could hardly refuse. Phillip knew she had not seen Bill and that she was supposed to be visiting him on his mother's behalf.

Sister Barnes led them to the ward.

Cherry was ice-cold with nerves as she walked beside her husband down the long, white hospital corridor to Bill's ward.

If the sight of Cherry and the sound of her voice restored his memory with Phillip there, it would be a catastrophe for her. The end of everything.

11

Cherry found herself at last at the side of Bill's bed. She looked down at him and longed to hold him in her arms. He lay motionless in his narrow bed; the clothes drawn up with that painful orderliness and smoothness which reeks of hospital discipline; his hands now listless; weak as a baby's.

One arm was in a sling. There was a white cap-bandage right over his head, hiding his hair. His face, in that ghastly frame, looked strange and unfamiliar; still pitifully sunbrowned. Her heart stood still as his eyes opened and looked straight into hers, and she wondered if he recognised her.

But no recognition dawned in those blue, handsome eyes. They were curiously blank.

Sister Barnes bent over him.

'Two more people who know you,

Mr. Carew,' she said softly. 'Try and remember — will you?'

Bill looked at Phillip and shook his head. He stared at Cherry. Cherry shivered with rage and jealousy as she saw him smile at the nurse. She saw too gratitude and friendliness in his eyes.

'Sorry, Sister. I don't remember either of them.'

'Speak to him, Cherry,' whispered Phillip.

She bit her lip. Trembling from head to foot with suppressed emotion, she bent over Bill.

'Bill,' she said. Her teeth chattered. 'Bill, don't you remember me, Cherry Brown, from Dalescombe.'

She half wanted him to remember, half dreaded it. But no light dawned in his eyes. He just gave her an apologetic smile.

'Sorry — I can't seem to remember you at all. Have I — known you long?'

Cherry could have wept aloud. She tried to control herself. But her voice shook as she answered him.

'Yes, for some years.'

He frowned, puzzled. Then he shook his head.

'I can't remember. It's horrible,' he groaned.

Sister Barnes put a hand on his pulse.

'All right, don't try and force it,' she said.

'My head hurts so,' he murmured.

Cherry forgot Phillip was there as she cried out:

'Bill, Bill, try to remember me!'

His face flushed painfully.

'In some vague way your face — your voice — are familiar — but I have no idea who you are.'

Sister Barnes looked at Cherry.

'You had better go, Miss Brown,' she whispered. 'He's getting upset and that won't do him any good.'

'Come along,' said Phillip, quite distressed by the scene. 'The poor chap can't remember anything. It's no good upsetting him, as Sister says.'

He took Cherry's arm and led her

away. She saw Bill sigh with relief and look up at Janet Barnes, smiling — the kind of smile he used to give Cherry when they first met. Cherry seethed with resentment. Bill had forgotten her, his adored Cherry; forgotten their love, their passion, and their marriage. Everything was new and strange to his clouded mind. Dark-eyed Sister Barnes who had special charge of him was his ministering angel. Cherry realised that if he stayed too long in hospital he would begin to love Janet Barnes.

She was torn with forebodings. She suffered real torment as Phillip led her away from Bill and out of the ward. She knew she was being punished for her sins. Bill was the only being on earth she ever cared for and now she was just a stranger to him. She felt a new kind of anguish — jealousy of another woman; something which had never happened before. She had always been so sure of herself — of her power to hold any man she chose.

But she kept silent. She dared not

give herself away; or Phillip, her first and real husband, might suspect that it was Bill, not he, she really loved.

Tears blinded her eyes as she walked down the corridor with Phillip. He glanced at her sharply:

'You seemed damned upset about that poor devil, Cherry,' he observed. 'Were you so keen about him as all that?'

'No, no,' she muttered, trying to control herself. 'But it was so pathetic, wasn't it?'

'Yes, for a man to lose his memory like that,' agreed Phillip. Then he added with a short laugh: 'Still he has the devil of a good-looking nurse. Quite the glamour girl. I could see he was smitten. Wonderful personality. What was her name? Barnes? Commonplace name — out of the common face.'

He could have said nothing more calculated to add to Cherry's despair, although he spoke without realising in the least what effect these words had on her. She choked back tears, and thought fiercely:

'She shan't get him — she shan't. He belongs to me. He is mine. Legally or illegally, he is mine. Our marriage certificate lies in my suitcase in the station hotel at this moment!'

Although she felt mad with nerves and worry, Cherry controlled herself as she returned to the hospital waiting-room with Phillip. He said:

'Look here, darling, why don't you come up to town now? I've got the car outside. I motored down to meet Frinton. If you like to meet me somewhere I'll drive you home once I've got rid of him.'

Cherry tried to collect her thoughts.

'All right,' she said dully. 'I've brought my suitcase from home. I intended going up to town as soon as I'd seen Bill. I'll wire to his mother from here.'

Phillip glanced at his wrist-watch.

'I'll just have a drink with Frinton. It's nearly twelve. I'll meet you at twelve-thirty. Say where?'

'Outside the station,' Cherry suggested.

Phillip hastily kissed her hand and whispered, 'Bye-bye, sweet.'

She left the hospital without seeing Mr. Frinton again. It was still raining dismally, but she did not notice the rain. She walked blindly down the wide stone steps of the hospital, down the wet street and towards her hotel.

Cherry's thoughts during the next thirty minutes were agonising. She had been very wicked and had practised a mean deception on two decent men. She had nothing to her credit except that she honestly loved Bill Carew and suffered very genuine grief at the turn events had taken. She might never see him again. He might not love her again or want her as he had before his accident.

She would never forget the touch of his lips — his wonderful, thrilling caresses. She could not get used to the fact that he did not remember her; that she was less than nothing to him now. It

183

seemed an impossible task to carry on, as if nothing had happened, with her married life with Phillip and remain sane.

Money, luxury, Le Touquet; a smart, gay holiday, in France held no attractions for her, although once it would have seemed immensely attractive. She was overcome with grief and worry. She wanted to go back and force Bill to remember her. She could not bear to think of him day and night in the care of Sister Jan Barnes, receiving the smiles that were once for Cherry. She would talk to him; comfort him; and maybe catch him on the rebound. He was a very handsome and lovable person. Cherry saw no reason why Janet Barnes should be unaware of that attraction and fail to respond to it.

Cherry wanted to go away and hide herself.

'Oh, God, Oh, God, I can't bear it!' she thought.

She would never be able to behave in a normal fashion; but she dared not lose Phillip as well as Bill. If she did lose them both there would be nothing left to live for.

Cherry managed to compose herself before she met Phillip. She was quite calm during the journey to London with him, laughing at his jokes, talking vivaciously. She became 'Mrs. Gerard' again. She had changed into a smart tie-silk dress, rubbed some rouge into her face (which was ghastly pale) outlined her lips generously with rose-coloured lipstick, and blackened her long lashes. She looked beautiful and glamorous. Phillip soon forgot about the scene in the Tunbridge Wells Hospital. When finally he mentioned it, it was only to speak of 'poor old Bill,' with sympathy and compassion; what a pity it would be if Bill Carew could never box again.

Phillip did not dream that under Cherry's mask of gaiety and nonchalance, her heart was filled with grief.

She managed to steel herself to bear the present total separation from Bill.

185

They flew to Le Touquet and booked at the biggest luxury hotel facing the blue sparkling sea.

They spent a few days there; then went on to Monte Carlo. There it was so bright and beautiful that she would not have been human if she had not felt a little happier.

Phillip was in the best of good humours. An old aunt, on his father's side had just died and left him a legacy of £20,000. He could afford to be more than usually generous. He bought her magnificent model dresses by Dior and Balmain; wonderful clips and a superb bracelet. He gave her money to waste in the Casino. He danced with her nightly. They ate at the most expensive restaurants. He delighted in showing her off. Cherry began to feel, in fact, rather like a dressed-up doll paraded for the benefit of the crowd.

They had a luxurious suite in the Hotel de Paris. Cherry had everything a woman could want — except love. Phillip gave her only passion. She tried to drown her conscience in his kisses, and gave him the semblance of passion in return. But *love*; real love and true affection were denied Cherry. She had left her heart behind her in a hospital ward with Bill Carew.

She tried not to think of him. But when she was not actually dancing or dining or playing 'Chemin' or sitting in the sun drinking aperitifs with Phillip, she was plunged into profound and unhappy thought. Torn with longing for Bill; with that new jealousy of Janet Barnes.

Often in the night Phillip awoke to find Cherry's face wet with tears. He would put an arm around her and say:

'Cherry, darling, my sweet, why are you crying? Aren't you happy with me? Is there anything you want I can buy for you?'

'Nothing, nothing that money can buy! Don't worry, I'm happy, Phillip. I was only dreaming . . . '

So the days and nights went by. Three weeks of gaiety in Monte Carlo, and she bathed every day and grew brown and more lovely than ever with that bloom of health and her new 'chic'.

Cherry really tried everything to stifle her passionate yearning for the man she really loved.

One day she found a book of Dowson's poems in a shop in Monte Carlo. She read a poem which seemed to fit her feelings.

'I have flung roses, roses riotously
   with the throng,
   Called for madder music, stron-
      ger wine.
But when the feast is finished and
   the lamps expire
Then falls thy shadow . . . and the
   night is thine.
   And I am weary and sick of an
      old passion.
   I have been faithful to thee, in
      my fashion!'

In between the bursts of feverish gaiety when she remembered Bill, she was indeed weary and sick. She was faithful to Bill . . . in her fashion!

How long could she go on? Cherry thought. How much longer could she endure this state of affairs? Would Bill's memory ever come back, and if so, would he still be in love with her?

12

Of course the day came when Phillip grew tired of hotel-life and the Riviera and seemed to wish to go home. At the same time Cherry was so thin and nervy that despite the golden tan he could see that she was not well. She was losing weight.

'Something is wrong, Cherry,' he said. 'Goodness knows what, my dear. You say you don't feel ill and yet — '

'I don't,' she interrupted him. 'I'm perfectly fit.'

'Well, you've lost all your curves,' Phillip grumbled, regarding her rather crossly. 'And I hate thin women.'

Cherry shrugged her shoulders. In the past such a speech would have hurt her. She would have been angry to think that Phillip only cared for her beauty and feared that she would lose her looks. He did not mind that she felt ill. It was impossible for her to explain to him that it was an illness of the mind that was ravaging her beauty. She was just pining for Bill. She slept badly and ate less and less. In consequence she lost that splendid look of health and strength and the dimples which used to make the old Cherry so irresistible.

Then suddenly, old Mr. Bellairs, Phillip's father died. He went suddenly of a coronary thrombosis and Phillip was called over to England to attend the old man's funeral. He left Cherry alone and she at once telephoned the hospital where Bill lay ill and inquired after him, only to hear that he was improving in health but his mental state remained the same. That was depressing enough. But when Phillip came back to Monte Carlo, Cherry found him changed for the worse. Now he was so rich. He had all that his heart could desire; his father's money — and freedom. In fact, Phillip Bellairs was an exceedingly rich man and he could do exactly what he wished. He no longer had any fear of being disinherited because of making a poor marriage.

From the hour of his return to Monte Carlo, a wall of coldness sprang up between Phillip and Cherry. She had never really loved him; only wanted his money. And now she did not even want that. It was Bill she desired without ceasing. She stopped being attractive to Phillip. She rarely made love to him in her old alluring way; made no effort to attract him. Suddenly he found her wooden and dull, far from charming. And he began to regret his marriage not a little.

His inheritance, too, seemed to alter his character. He grew more than ever selfish and vain. His conceit made Cherry feel quite sick. He imagined there was nobody on earth like Phillip Bellairs and he never allowed Cherry to forget that she had held a domestic job when he married her. At times she was maddened and goaded into fits of temper and hot resentment. At other times she snapped her fingers in his face and told him she didn't care a jot for him.

Now and then, inflamed by champagne, Phillip came to her room in a soft and passionate mood and tried to make love to her; to show her her old hot lover. Then Cherry hated him more than ever. She preferred him to remain cold. His caresses nauseated her now. She felt no longer able to act a part. She wanted Bill . . . Oh, God! how she wanted him.

No more was Cherry the old gay light-hearted girl. She soon turned into a sullen, brooding, morose young woman . . . harder in a way . . . yet infinitely softer in her thoughts of Bill Carew. What wouldn't she have done for him? What wouldn't she have suffered for one of his old smiles and kisses?

Phillip, to make things worse, decided to travel. To take her further and further from Bill. They toured the blue, glittering Mediterranean coast, and the mountains in France and Italy.

Then he rented a villa in Ville-franche from a French Marquis who was a friend of his. It was a wonderful house, full of carved pillars; marble floors; hand-painted ceilings and priceless Italian furniture. The gardens were glorious; leading down to the edge of the sea. From the white terraces one could see the whole lovely panorama; Mentone; Monaco; Nice. They had the Marquis's excellent staff and they served their English patrons with exquisitely cooked meals. Phillip also had the use of the Marquis's Lagonda, and he liked to drive along the Côte d'Azur with Cherry, beautiful and chic, beside him.

If Phillip amused himself with other women, Cherry neither knew nor cared. But mostly, he spent his time in the Casino. Gambling was a vice with him, and now that he had plenty of money he played baccarat and roulette half the day and most of the night. He played with Farouk one night, and boasted that he won money from the ex-King of Egypt.

He didn't want Cherry with him often and she stayed at home in the villa, quite alone; the 'poor, little rich girl'. She was terribly lonely and breaking her heart for Bill. All the luxury and splendour of these days bored Cherry to death. With Bill at her side, she would have been madly happy! But he was in England, in hospital still, and he did not even remember she existed.

October came. Phillip showed no desire to return to England. The Marquis made it possible for them to remain in Villefranche, so they stayed on in the villa. By this time they had ceased to be 'Mr. and Mrs. Gerard'. There was no longer any need for the secrecy. Phillip had his father's money. He wrote to his mother and announced that he was married and would bring his wife to see his family on his return. But Cherry told herself, with some irony, that Phillip would keep her out here a long time before he would 'show her off' to his family and friends in England. She even toyed with the idea of running away — going back to Tunbridge Wells and Bill. But she could not afford to leave him.

In those days when she really suffered, she tried to expiate a little of her wrong-doing by being good to those who had brought her up and always cared for her. Phillip did not care what she did so long as she never involved him in her humble family. She let her mother and sisters know that she had married Phillip and sent them as many presents by air as she could. Although Phillip was no longer interested in Cherry, he was not mean to her, and she sent her mother as much money as Phillip could arrange from his London bank. She bought beautiful clothes for her two sisters, which she knew would delight their simple hearts. Cherry became the idol of the Brown family, and that was some consolation to her sore and aching heart.

Through Polly she heard that Bill had

not returned to Little Cross but was still in hospital. So she presumed that he was still in the charge of the brown-eyed Janet. Only when she thought of Janet Barnes, she became the old, vicious, unscrupulous Cherry. She loathed the idea of Janet Barnes being with Bill all day. She wept when she thought of him lying helpless in that hospital ward.

Then the dreary, empty round of pleasure in the south of France, ended abruptly.

Phillip came to Cherry's bedroom one morning when she was drinking her early cup of tea and reading an English newspaper. He said that he wanted to talk to her. He so rarely came into her bedroom (they had agreed to have separate rooms) that Cherry was vaguely surprised. She sat up and looked at him.

'You're very early,' she said, glowering at him through her long lashes.

'Tell the servants to prepare two bedrooms.'

'Two?' she repeated, staring at him. 'Oh. Have you visitors coming?'

'Yes,' said Phillip. Cherry thought he looked at her with slightly malicious amusement. He began to walk restlessly up and down the room, hands in the pocket of the gorgeous black padded satin dressing-gown which he was wearing. He was, as usual, immaculately turned out; his head sleek; his appearance that of a wealthy 'playboy'. But she disliked him ... cordially disliked him. She said:

'Who are the guests?'

'Bill Carew and that nurse who was in charge of him — Sister Barnes,' he said.

If Phillip had flung a bomb at Cherry's feet she could not have been more startled or shaken. The blood rushed to her head. Her heart pounded ... so madly that she thought she would faint. She sat very still, struggling for composure. In the gilt mirror opposite her bed she could see her reflection ... a thin, fragile figure in pale blue chiffon bedjacket . . . a face thinned and quite spiritualised by suffering . . . the agony of longing through which she had passed for so many weeks . . . a face golden-brown yet hollow-cheeked — hazel eyes enormous, circled with violet shadows.

Cherry said faintly:

'*Bill Carew . . . coming here?*'

'Yes,' Phillip replied as he lit a cigarette. He put it carefully in a long holder and placed it between his teeth. 'Your old friend from home, my dear.'

'But why?' Cherry asked. 'Why have you invited them?'

'Not to amuse you,' he said with that touch of malice. 'To amuse myself. I wrote to his manager the other day and the fellow says Bill is quite well: his collar-bone healed and his constitution unimpaired. His memory has not returned, but his physique apparently is as magnificent as ever. His trainer thinks if he has a month's complete rest and good food, etc., he will be as fit to box as he ever was. It amuses me to promote a big boxing-match and I've always believed in young Carew. He'll be a champion one day. So I've asked him here. Villa Psyche is an excellent place for him to recuperate in.'

'I see,' Cherry said calmly. But her heart was still galloping and her thoughts chaotic. She quite saw why Phillip had invited Bill to stay. He had always wanted the thrill of backing a champion. If he thought Bill would box again, he would do anything for him. She was wildly excited at the idea of seeing Bill again . . . more thrilled and wide-awake than she had been for weeks. At the same time she was terrified. If his memory returned while he was here . . . if he recognised her . . . remember she *married him* in Tunbridge Wells . . .

But all she said was:

'I am glad he's coming and that he is better. But why the nurse — must she come too?'

'Yes, for two reasons,' said Phillip. 'First, Carew's left arm has to be massaged and this girl appears to be a first-rate masseuse as well as a trained nurse; secondly, she is taking her annual holiday from the hospital and Frinton suggested she should come with her patient, continue the massage and have her holiday at the same time. She seemed charming, I thought, and it would be nice to let her come here.'

Cherry could have bitten her tongue through with rage and jealousy in that moment. All the way along, the almond-eyed Janet had given her a strange impression that she would play some sort of a part in Bill's life. She had had that presentiment.

Now here she was coming with Bill . . . to be his daily companion; to fly over to France with him.

Phillip noticed the peculiar look on Cherry's face, and came to her bedside. He looked down at her with a smile that held more scorn than affection.

'Feeling sore, Cherry? Afraid your old admirer might start a romance with his pretty nurse? Come, come

. . . you're a married woman now
. . . not a moon-struck domestic
hanging round Dalescombe Woods
with her boy-friend.'

She could have struck him across his
cruel, sneering mouth. With difficulty
she restrained herself; managed to force
an answering jibe:

'I wonder you're not jealous of
throwing me into the company of an
'old admirer' as you call our handsome
boxer.'

'I'm not jealous of *you*, dear Cherry,'
he drawled. 'Besides which Carew has
forgotten who you are. He won't worry
his head over you. You're not so
devastating as you used to be, believe
me.'

Cherry sprang from the bed, flung a
satin dressing-gown over her trembling
figure. Her face was white with passion.
She said between her teeth:

'*You* may not find me charming, but
other man might. I don't put myself out
to attract *you* any more.'

He laughed at her outburst. Then his

spoiled, sensual face grew stern.

'Don't forget that you're my wife,' he said shortly. 'And while you bear my name, you'll do me the kindness of behaving as my wife should behave . . . not like Miss Brown of Dalescombe Cottages. Kindly retain your dignity when Carew and his nurse arrive.'

Cherry found his insults unbearable that morning. She burst into tears and pushed him out of her room and told him to go to hell. All that was ill-bred in Cherry rose uppermost. She didn't want to be dignified and she wasn't.

But after he had gone she remembered that to-day Bill was coming to Villa Psyche. She told herself, feverishly, that she must look her best for him. He might not know her . . . but she made up her mind then and there to attract him; to win him all over again. He had adored her, once. She still adored him. Frantic with longing she determined to use all her wiles to revive that passion which could not be dead in his heart even although his brain was sleeping.

'What chance has Janet Barnes against me,' Cherry thought. 'She is an unsophisticated girl, and cannot compete against me.' She would be a fish out of water in this villa; awkward, badly-dressed.

Cherry vowed that Janet Barnes should fail dismally in comparison with her in this villa. And that, no matter what the consequence might be, to make Phillip eat his words . . . to show him that she was still devastating, and still capable of making men mad about her. And Bill should be one of these men.

13

Cherry never forgot the hour when Bill and Sister Barnes arrived.

The Lagonda brought them from the airport.

She waited for them in the drawing-room; a long, lovely room with satin-panelled walls; a gilded ceiling painted with cupids; rare old satinwood cabinets full of priceless china; long windows draped with heavy gold satin curtains, looking out over the exquisite garden where the cypress trees were etched against the matchless blue of the sea.

She had spent hours in her bedroom with her French personal maid, Gabrielle. She had rushed out to the most expensive shop in Monte Carlo, early in the morning, to buy a new dress . . . new shoes . . . a new perfume. She had taken more pains than she had done for weeks, to look beautiful and her mirror told her she had succeeded. She was still thin, but wore one of those wonderful simple and expensive dresses from Jacques Greef. Tie-silk, deep green with black figures, with a little tight bodice and full pleated skirt. With it she wore a gold necklace and long gold earrings. Her chestnut hair had been washed and set and perfumed by Gabrielle. It curled crisply over her head. Her eyes were brilliant with excitement, her tanned face radiant. Today she was beautiful again and nobody could deny it. Her long slim legs were bare and brown and she wore black sandals tied around her tiny ankles.

Bill walked into the salon. As he came Cherry heard Janet Barnes in the hall, saying:

'You go and say hello to Mrs. Bellairs, Bill. I'll follow when I've got my bag. They've left it in the car.'

The room seemed to spin round Cherry as Bill walked down the long room across the polished floor toward her. As through a mist she saw him ... tall, much thinner since his accident, but as handsome as ever ... even more handsome with the refinement of illness ... face unusually pale; eyes darkly blue; hair black and curling; mouth and chin as resolute. He looked at her. Cherry's heart seemed to stand still. Would he know her now?

But Bill did not recognise her. To him Cherry was a strange being ... beautiful in her green and black silky dress, with the Southern sunshine falling goldenly upon her through the open windows.

'How do you do,' he said. 'You are — Mrs. Bellairs?'

'Yes,' Cherry managed the word somehow.

He shook hands with her formally. For a moment in the most anguished silence she looked up at him, and thought her control would go. She longed to feel his arms about her; to feel that resolute, well-shaped mouth on hers . . . to hear him say as he had said in old days: 'My sweet Cherry, oh *Darling!*'

She knew she was nothing to him . . . that he was not the least affected by the idea of her marriage . . . whereas in the past he would have half-killed her in jealous passion.

She dared not hold out her arms as she longed to do; to say, '*Bill, darling, don't you remember?*'

He looked round the room.

'What a marvellous place,' he said. 'Like a film-set. It's awfully kind of you and your husband to let me come and convalesce here . . . frightfully good of you both.'

'Not at all,' Cherry gulped.

Then Sister Barnes joined them. She advanced, rather shyly . . . looking perfectly sweet and quite attractively dressed, in a grey tailored suit with a little burnt straw hat on her dark head. Cherry hid her jealousy as she watched Janet come toward her. Forcing a smile on her lips she said graciously:

208

'Welcome to Villa Psyche, Sister.'

Janet Barnes looked staggered when she recognised Cherry. She had no idea that Mrs. Bellairs would be the girl whom she had last seen in Tunbridge Wells crazy with anxiety about Bill. She stared at Cherry, in frank amazement; then slowly held out her hand.

'How do you do,' she said. 'It's so very good of you to let me come with Mr. Carew.

'Not at all,' Cherry replied. 'Delighted. The last time we met I was — not married.'

Her grave, almond-brown eyes still stared at Cherry. She was astonished. Cherry had seemed so madly in love with Bill, in Tunbridge Wells . . . secretly engaged to him. And now she was married — Mrs. Bellairs, her wealthy hostess.

Bill wandered to the window to examine the view and Cherry seized her opportunity. She leaned forward and whispered to Miss Barnes:

'I can't explain, but please keep my

secret. I am married now . . . and Bill does not remember me so it can't upset him.'

She looked at Cherry gravely.

'No — he does not remember — it can't hurt him. You can trust me to say nothing, Mrs. — er — Bellairs.'

Cherry saw that Janet despised her as a girl who had consoled herself rapidly with a wealthy man.

A look of relief sprang into Janet Barnes' dark eyes when she heard what Cherry had to say. She was glad Cherry was married . . . glad that Bill was free to love again.

Bill turned from the window.

'Isn't this a glorious spot, Jan?' he said.

Jan smiled in agreement. Cherry saw that Janet was more than fond of Bill. She shivered with impotent passion and rage. Helpless to say anything . . . do anything. And then she saw Bill smile back at Jan Barnes. In that exchange of looks a whole history was revealed. His blue eyes literally caressed her. *He was in love with her*. Cherry knew it beyond all doubt . . . and later it was proved to her. Her solicitude for him — her gentleness; her grave beauty had had a natural effect on an injured man. She had become his ideal of womanhood. She was a lovable person, who would appeal very strongly to a man like Bill.

Cherry knew, too, the fascination of Bill. Few women could resist those Irish eyes of his; that attractive voice; that unique strength and vitality which he normally possessed and was now recovering. Jan would not be the type to give her heart easily, but she found it easy to give it to Bill Carew.

They were in love. Cherry watched them smile and talk to each other, and knew that before their holiday ended they would announce their engagement.

The rest of the day was torment for Cherry.

Phillip came home. He was most charming to the pretty nurse who relaxed in the atmosphere of Villa

Psyche and was natural and gay. He was nice to Bill. They talked boxing; they smoked and drank together. They became quite friendly. Cherry watched them ironically. A short time ago they would never have sat opposite each other smoking and drinking. They would have been primitive enemies; hating each other. They had both loved and wanted Cherry Brown.

She could hardly drag her burning gaze from Bill's face. She wondered what would happen if he suddenly recovered his memory. Would he go back to the old hot love for her? Would this present penchant for Janet flicker out like a feeble flame? But she realised with despair that it would be disastrous for Bill to remember. The truth would come out; her duplicity would be revealed. He would loathe her and Phillip would want a divorce. She might be committed for trial as a bigamist.

She had never been more utterly miserable and afraid. Sometimes Bill talked in a friendly casual fashion to his beautiful hostess. But he seemed barely interested. His eyes merely glanced at Cherry, indifferently; then away again. It was upon Janet Barnes that his eyes continually rested . . . to her that he spoke in the caressing voice that Cherry remembered only too well.

Although Cherry could scarcely bear to smile she acted the part of a charming hostess. She wore a mask of indifference and gaiety. But underneath it all she was torn to pieces. It was monstrous, she thought, that Bill should no longer feel attracted to her; that her allure and charm should leave him so cold. She could not, would not, believe that Jan Barnes had so completely usurped her place in his affections.

Towards the end of the evening Cherry was so worked up that she acted crazily . . . recklessly. She was determined at all costs to make Bill realise, if only for a moment that he loved her. She was determined to feel his arms crushing her, his lips on hers. She was parched . . . hungry . . . starving for his love. She could no longer stand his treatment of her.

They all sat in the drawing-room, facing the open windows. They could see the moonlit terrace; the purple sea, glittering in the starlight. A perfect Mediterranean night! Phillip had put a record on the gramophone . . . a soft, lilting rumba from South America.

Jan looked quite beautiful in a simple grey lace dress. She stood by the fireplace to examine a rare painting. She was an artist herself. Phillip stood next to her.

Bill was still sitting beside Cherry. He had just finished a whisky and soda and lit a cigarette. Cherry looked at him with despairing eyes. He seemed not to be aware of her as a woman. Yet she was ten times more beautiful than Jan . . . at her very best in a wonderful dinner gown of black organza and lace with a low neck; three rows of milky pearls; a spray of orchids; big drop earrings and small black satin shoes. Perfumed

. . . alluring, with her golden tan and big languorous eyes with their painted blue lids. Most men would have found her irresistible. Yet Bill had eyes only for the young nurse talking 'art' with Phillip.

All that was mad, bad and reckless rose uppermost in Cherry. She sprang to her feet.

'Come, Bill, let me show you our garden by moonlight,' she said, lightly.

'I should love to see it Mrs. Bellairs,' he said politely.

He followed her into the garden. Janet followed them with her brown eyes, gravely, wonderingly. Phillip frowned and then shrugged his shoulders and continued chatting to Jan. But she went on, completely enslaved by the most passionate and desperate desire to regain the love of Bill Carew, who had once so loved and wanted her.

She took him down to the moonlit terrace; to the shadow of a tall cypress; she leaned against the balustrade and looked up at him . . . knowing that she looked beautiful with the moonlight in her eyes and on her bare tanned throat and shoulders and arms. She said in a low husky voice:

'Bill, you must call me Cherry. Don't let's be formal, Bill. I can't believe that you remember nothing at all about our former friendship.'

He flushed and looked rather embarrassed.

'I'm terribly sorry,' he said. 'But I . . . just can't remember . . . the past at all. It's a total loss.'

'Not the old days in Dalescombe?' Cherry asked, breathing hard and fast . . . 'when you took me to Dalescombe Woods . . . oh, Bill.'

He put a hand to his head. Cherry saw that he felt nothing but distress.

'I assure you, I don't remember a thing,' he said awkwardly.

Tears rushed to Cherry's eyes. She put her hands on his shoulders; drew nearer to him; shivering, burning.

'Bill, Bill . . . try and remember

216

. . . you loved me, *yes, you loved me* . . . that night in the woods . . . when you kissed me . . . held me . . . called me your own Cherry. You shall remember . . . Bill, hold me now . . . kiss me again . . . I'll make you remember . . . *Bill!*'

Panting, sobbing, crazy with desire, she flung herself into his arms.

14

Bill instinctively put his arms around that slim figure — but not in response to her passionate appeal — only because she had literally flung herself against him. He held her away from him and stared down at her, his face white and amazed.

'Mrs. Bellairs — Cherry!' he exclaimed. Cherry could see that he was both astonished and shocked. 'Please — '

'Oh, Bill,' she broke in, sobbing wildly. 'Do try to remember. I am your Cherry. You cannot have forgotten . . . Dalescombe Woods . . . the nightingales singing . . . our wonderful love. Darling, darling, don't you remember what you did just before your accident? That Saturday morning in Tunbridge Wells?'

She could feel his strong body shake. But not with desire for her. Only with nerves and embarrassment. Something gnawed at Bill's consciousness ... some dim, shadowy shape of remembrance worried him as he held Cherry's beautiful form and stared down at her, at the tears glittering in the moonlight on her ravaged face. But he shook his head.

'No, I remember nothing of that. Is it possible that I — that you!' he broke off, his face scarlet. He was distressed and puzzled. But he felt no love for Cherry in his heart. To him she was a stranger. Her tears, her passionate pleading were repugnant to him. Her heart was broken. She made a last, desperate appeal to break through that dreadful blank wall in his brain.

'Bill,' she choked, 'kiss me ... darling ... let my kisses help you to remember!'

He pushed her gently but firmly from him. His hot colour had faded and left him quite ashen.

'Look, my dear, you forget,' he said. 'This is not possible. Whatever we were to each other in the past you are married. I am your guest — your husband's guest.'

Cherry clenched her hands.

'Before Phil . . . before that . . . I belonged to you, Bill, and you to me.'

'No, no, surely not — ' the big man blushed scarlet. Honest and clean-living and single of heart, he was shocked and repelled by Cherry's mad outburst. How well she knew Bill. Although he lost his memory he had lost none of his finest characteristics and she knew it. She was a married woman and his hostess. He was disgusted by her conduct. She, on her part, had lost all power to sweep this man off his feet. It was a bitter blow to Cherry.

She stood silent for a moment, a handkerchief pressed to her streaming eyes. Bill found a cigarette and lit it. His fingers shook. He smoked furiously for a moment, then looked at Cherry under his lids. He was distressed beyond words. Then he broke out:

'I'm more sorry than I can say. Please, do let us forget this. Wipe it right out.'

She flung back her head and gave him a long, bitter look.

'You've certainly forgotten everything,' she said. 'Once you loved me better than anything on earth. Do you doubt it? Do you find it repulsive now?'

He took the cigarette from his lips and lowered his gaze.

'Far from it,' he said with sincerity. 'I think you are absolutely beautiful — and really you have been swell to me, and so kind to have me here. But I don't remember that we — that there was anything between us and I — don't really want to remember. You are Bellair's wife — dash it all.'

'I see,' Cherry smothered a wild laugh. 'You are — too moral.'

'I hope I am decent enough not to make love to a married woman,' he said, looking quite pathetically awkward.

Cherry pressed clenched hands to

her forehead. It was burning. She felt one great flame of humiliation. She could not make Bill remember . . . and he did not want to remember, because she was Phillip's wife. She realized what a fool she had been to chain herself to Phillip for his money. The money and luxury of Villa Psyche sickened her. She was stifled by it all. She wanted the old love and the innocent fun with Bill, but he was lost to her. She lost all sense of proportion, of delicacy, and screamed at him:

'You are mad to think you were never in love with me, Bill. You would change your tune if I could show you a certain document up in my bedroom — something to prove to you just how much you do belong to me still!'

He flung away his half-smoked cigarette and looked at her with distasteful eyes.

'I don't understand,' he said. 'To what document are you referring?'

Cherry dared not tell him or show him that marriage certificate . . . proof of her wretched bigamy. She began to sob again.

'I suppose you think that stupid hospital nurse is more attractive than I am. Dear Sister Barnes has taken my place in your heart and — '

'Please, Mrs. Bellairs,' Bill interrupted. His eyes flashed. 'Don't bring *her* name into this.'

'Is it so precious to you?' Cherry flung at him.

'It *is* — most precious,' he said quietly. 'Jan is one of the finest, nicest girls I've ever met. I hope one day soon when I've made my way, to ask her to marry me.'

That broke Cherry entirely. She gave a low cry and flung herself down on a marble seat which overlooked the starlit Mediterranean. All around them was the beauty, the romance of the South, the warmth and scent and languor of a Riviera night. For Cherry none of that glamour existed. She was lost in a bitter, frightful world of her own . . . the bitterness of regret. She laid her beautiful head on folded arms and cried brokenly.

The sight of this lovely chic young woman's violent grief — lack of control, appalled Bill. He touched her bare shoulder. She shuddered under his hand. His fingers filled her with unspeakable desire for their past shared passion.

'Please, Mrs. Bellairs — Cherry — don't cry — I'm sorry if I have hurt you — if we — if there was some sort of love between us,' he stammered. 'But you have married someone else. It's not my fault if it's all ended now between us, is it? Anyhow, I tell you frankly — I care very much for Jan. I hope — '

'Oh, go away, go away,' she interrupted. 'I can't bear any more.'

'Then I'll clear off,' he said. 'And please remember I'll not say a word to a living soul about this. I'll forget it absolutely and you must forget it too. Do let us wipe it right out.'

So polite, so generous . . . yet so cold. Like a glacier. Bill, who had once known a volcanic passion for Cherry.

'*Wipe it right out,*' he said. How little he understood! How little he realised what an appalling situation it was for Cherry Bellairs — nee Brown. How difficult it would be to 'wipe it right out.' She had committed bigamy. She had married William David Carew on the Saturday morning of his accident. That could never be wiped out. And one day if he went back to Tunbridge Wells (which he obviously would do) to get a license to marry Jan he would be told that he was already married to Miss Cherry Brown. What then?

It was a ghastly prospect. A calamity of the first water, and Cherry was forced to admit that the fault was hers. She had plunged into a labyrinth of lies and intrigue. Now it was for her to find her way out alone. Terribly alone. No longer loved by Bill. No longer cared for even by Phillip.

She lifted her head from her arms. Her eyelids were puffy with violent weeping. She took a mirror and powder puff from an exquisite Petit Point bag which she was carrying. She looked at her face and shivered. What a red, patchy, disfigured face, drenched with tears. She tried to 'make up' and failed. She realised she had better go in to the villa; straight to her bedroom and tell Bill to let Phillip know that she was ill and had gone to bed.

She staggered rather than walked through the flower-filled garden to the villa. Bill hung around; reluctant to leave his mysterious and disconcerting hostess in this state. He gave her a quick, nervous look.

'Won't you come with me?'

'No. Tell my husband that I have a bad headache.'

'I am so sorry,' Bill said, with cold courtesy. 'Good-night.'

'Good-night,' Cherry replied mechanically.

Somehow Cherry managed to get to her room unnoticed — she tore off the pearls, her orchids, her wonderful dinner gown which she had bought especially to excite Bill's admiration. She flung them away and slipped on a dressing-gown and sat in front of the open window. Her slight body burned as though with fever. She could not cry any more, but could only look at the starry magical Mediterranean night and wonder what further punishment Fate had in store for her. Nothing could be worse than Bill's ice-cold rejection. His complete indifference to her. His confessed love for another woman.

'How can I bear it,' she kept on whispering to herself through dry, cracked lips. 'I want you back, Bill. I want you back.'

She had always loved him. She felt she would go mad if she could not win him back — even now.

How long she sat there, she did not know. It might have been an hour . . . two hours. Phillip, and his guests stayed talking downstairs. The maid, Gabrielle, who had not expected Cherry to come up to bed so soon, was with the other servants, and she was quite alone. And never before had she felt so lonely.

Then, under the window she heard voices. She leaned out and could just distinguish in the shadows, two people who stood together on the terrace below. She switched off the light and plunged the room into darkness so that she could see without being seen. She watched and strained her ears. For those two people were Bill and Janet Barnes. They were alone, talking together. They were close, close to each other.

Cherry wondered viciously what they had to say. She was fiendishly glad when they unconsciously moved nearer the window ... paused just below, without realising that they were being overlooked and heard.

A shaft of pale, pure moonlight falling through the dark shadows of the cypress trees, shone upon Bill's dark head, and the girl's darker one. They were facing each other, leaning a little against the white balustrade. Cherry could see even their expressions; hers slightly questioning. And his was the face of the old Bill she had once known. Passionate and admiring. He was in love with his nurse. For her, all his tenderness, his burning ardour that once had been for Cherry alone.

Cherry knelt by her window . . . loathing those two yet unable to tear her gaze from them. Suffering, yet fascinated, she watched and listened.

Bill's voice reached her . . .

'It's marvellous in this superb villa, isn't it, Jan?'

'Wonderful,' she agreed softly. 'So full of beauty that it makes one want to cry, Bill . . . after the sights and sounds in hospital.'

'My poor little nurse — you work damned hard too. Remember I've watched you for weeks. I shall never forget the hours of devotion you gave me. You saved my life, Jan.'

'No — I can't take the credit for that, my dear,' she replied. 'Your life was never in danger.'

'Anyhow, I would like to offer that life in return for all that kindness,' he said eagerly.

Cherry bit her lip till blood came. She suffered the pangs of the dying. An hour ago he had looked at her with cold distaste . . . rejected her.

She could not take her gaze from Bill and Jan. She knelt there, shivering, tortured, eaten up with jealousy and despair.

'Jan, darling,' Bill said, 'my angel of goodness, will you marry me? I love you, darling. I think I loved you from the first hour I woke up in that hospital bed and saw you looking down at me and felt your fingers on my wrist. Jan, look at me, sweet. Do you love me, too?'

Cherry saw passion spring into Jan's dark eyes; saw love transform her face to rare beauty. And she could have killed her before she did what she did, then . . . she put her arms around Bill's neck and said:

'Of course I love you, Bill. I'm just as

crazy about you as I can be. You're my ideal, darling. But are you sure there is no one else in your life — that life you don't remember?'

He took her in his arms and said:

'Nobody that I wish to remember anyhow. There will never be anybody now but you, my angel.'

'Angel.' The name he had once used for Cherry. She nearly shouted down at him to tell him to stop.

'Bill, Bill,' she wanted to scream at him, 'it isn't true. There is me, your Cherry.'

But she dared not. Cold, numb with a sensation of frightful despair, she watched Bill gather Janet's tall, slim figure close to his heart; their lips met in a long, ardent kiss. She could look no more. It hurt too cruelly. She sank into a little huddled heap on the floor.

If ever a woman was punished for duplicity; for greed, for any of the sins that had been hers, Cherry Bellairs was punished in that hour.

15

Later that same night, Cherry came to a new decision. Bill, for the moment, was lost to her. The best thing for her to do was to regain Phillip's affections, otherwise she would find herself falling between two stools. If Bill was deeply in love with his young nurse and contemplated early marriage, there was the terrible danger of his discovering from the registrar in Tunbridge Wells that he had married Cherry. That would ruin her altogether. It could not separate her much more completely from Bill, but it could and would drive Phillip from Cherry for ever. He could even put her in prison if he wished — for bigamy. The pair of them could punish her nicely, she reflected, if they chose to be vindictive. She might find herself flung out of Phillip's house and left alone in the world, disgraced and penniless. Her own humble family would not welcome back such a Cherry.

She told herself, feverishly, that as she had forfeited the only real love she had ever known she had better turn to the other man she had wanted to marry. Cherry knew it would not be easy. Phillip and she had been estranged for weeks. He had grown tired of her indifference to him; she had made no attempt to beguile him in her old, fascinating fashion.

Cherry told herself that she had better win Phillip back again; make him settle some money on her legally (a thing he had not yet done) then induce him to take her right away, to South America, or Canada . . . anywhere, out of Europe and away from the danger of her sin being discovered by Bill.

She visualised herself going abroad with her husband; starting a new life; perhaps having a child and finding new happiness and hitherto unknown ideals. She had never contemplated mother-hood. But she considered it now. She thought she might regain a little of her lost happiness in a baby of her own; might even grow fond of Phillip, escape the ultimate calamity which must fall on her if she remained in Europe. It would only be torture — physical and mental — to remain where she could see or hear of Bill and Jan. She must anyhow try to seduce Phillip from his plan of making a boxing-champion out of Bill Carew.

All these resolutions crowded on her at once and she wallowed in them. She became thrilled with the prospect of escaping misery and tragedy and of making a new and better life. She was sick of intrigue and weary of passion. She had had enough.

Cherry decided to begin her campaign right away — that very night.

By the time Phillip came upstairs — it was long past midnight, for he was always late — she had bathed; perfumed her bright, silky curls and brushed them into a shining halo about her small classic head. She put on her loveliest night-gown — pearl grey chiffon with cherry-coloured ribbons. Cherry — her name — and a floating grey lace negligée over this.

With all traces of tears and misery erased from her face — beautiful and alluring as the old Cherry, she strolled into her husband's bedroom which communicated with hers. She was satisfied that she looked her best.

Phillip was in bed, reading a book by the light of a green shaded lamp on the table beside him. He stared at Cherry, in profound astonishment. It was so long since she had gone into his room and he rarely entered hers. He gave her a cursory look from head to foot, then that sneering look which she had grown to hate, crossed his thin, dark face.

'Is this a mannequin show and you showing 'monsieur' the latest model in night attire?' he said.

Cherry's heart beat jerkily. She tried to echo his laugh. She hated him. Yet she wanted to win him back; to prove she had not lost her power to attract him. She walked across the room — drew the Venetian blinds, then seated herself on the edge of his bed and crossed slim tanned legs.

'I've come for a chat, Phil darling,' she said.

'Phil, *darling*, eh?' he laughed shortly. 'Want a cheque?'

'No,' Cherry tried hard to keep her temper. 'Something less mercenary than that. Phillip, I've been thinking that we are not very happy together these days and I — I want you to help me to put matters right.'

'Oh!' he said. He laid down his novel and regarded her with a kind of malicious amusement in his narrow eyes. 'And what do you wish me to do, my dear?'

'Our relations with each other. I — I want us to be friends again,' she stammered.

'We *are* friends, so far as I know, and much happier nowadays than when we were hanging on to each other's apron-strings.'

'No,' Cherry said. Suddenly she threw herself into his arms and clasped her hands about his neck. She hid her burning face on his chest. 'Phillip,' she whispered. 'My dear, I want you to love me again and I want to love you. Oh, Phillip, let's begin all over again.' She really fancied in that moment she wanted to feel Phillip's arms about her, and know his love was still hers.

Phillip did not move a muscle. He did not touch or kiss her. After a second, she looked up at him and saw that he was *smiling* . . . yes, smiling in a cold, cruel, evil kind of way.

'Phillip,' she gasped. 'Don't look like that. You haven't lost all your feeling for me, surely, Phillip — can't we begin again?'

He took her hands and flung them away. He said in a hard, sneering voice:

'I'm afraid we can't. It's much too late. I did love you once. I was infatuated, anyhow, shall we say and was dam' fool enough to marry you very speedily. I regret it now. It isn't any too pleasant for a man in my position to have a girl like you for a wife. However, we must make the best of that. So long as you behave yourself decently I'll go on living in the same house with you and giving you money to spend. But that's as far as it goes. No more of the sob-stuff, please. I don't want to make love to you and I'm quite sure you don't really want me to. If it's a new toy of some kind, I'll buy it for you to-morrow. We'll run over to Cannes, if you like.

That cold, calculated speech stung cruelly. She realised with despair that her husband was as impervious to her beauty and charm as Bill had been earlier in the evening. Both the men she had wanted and once had won, had ceased to care for her. She was forced to face the bitter, humiliating truth. She had failed with Bill, and with Phillip. A low cry escaped her lips:

'I did really want us to begin again ... I'm most unhappy ... and lonely ... '

'Rubbish,' said Phillip. Then he yawned. 'You're a bit het-up — too much champagne, my dear. My advice to you is to get to bed and sleep it off. Goodnight.'

Cherry stared at him with real misery in her eyes. He yawned again and returned to his book. She ceased to exist for him.

She got up and stumbled back to her bedroom. She flung herself on her bed and lay face downwards, arms outspread, crucified by the bitter and passionate despair that consumed her that night.

Neither of these two men who had once wanted her so passionately wanted her now. She was nothing to either of them. And she no longer had any hope of regaining even a little happiness with Phillip . . . no hope of having a child. She had absolutely nothing but money. And she realised in that dreadful hour how little money counted without love.

The punishment of Cherry Brown

was far from completed. It had only just begun.

A terrible, unforgettable day dawned for her. She had not slept all night. She felt a mental and physical wreck. But somehow she managed to make up her face and put on a smart white sharkskin suit and appear in front of her guests, smiling as though she had not a care in the world.

Jan Barnes — radiant with new-found love, had eyes only for Bill. Bill, equally happy, had eyes only for her. Phillip appeared to be interested, as usual, only in himself. Cherry tried to laugh and talk and hide the hideous misery — and fear — which she was feeling.

Bill avoided Cherry, but she still loved him, wanted him. When common decency forced him to speak to her, he was just studiously polite.

At midday Phillip suggested a run to Cannes in the Lagonda. He wanted to drive it himself. Bill and Jan fell in readily with this plan. Cherry said

'Anything you like.' She felt that nothing mattered any more.

They set out in the Lagonda along the white, dusty road in a blaze of hot sunshine. Bill and Jan sat in the back, holding hands. Cherry sat beside Phillip in a state of deep dejection.

Then the accident happened . . . only a slight one and they all escaped serious injury by a sheer miracle . . . Phillip turned a hairpin bend in reckless haste; another car, a big American Cadillac rounded on them; Phillip swerved to avoid it and they crashed into a stone wall and turned over. They were all flung out of the car.

Cherry hit her head, and lost consciousness for a moment. When she came to her senses she was sitting in the middle of the road, and Bill was near her, rubbing his head from which the blood was streaming. Phillip, who appeared to be only bruised and shaken was helping Janet to her feet. The young nurse had escaped with a few bruises.

Cherry looked dazedly at Bill. He

stared at her. Then suddenly he gave her a bewildered kind of smile and held out both hands:

'Cherry — little Cherry,' he muttered.

Her heart leaped with joy. The world seemed bright. Bill's memory had returned. The second blow to his head, and a far less serious one than the first, had in some strange way restored all that had been sleeping in his brain. He knew her ... he just slipped back naturally into the past.

16

The excitement and danger of that moment was so intense that Cherry remained speechless. She sat stupidly in the road, staring at Bill. He — bruised and shaken — got on to his feet and hurried over to her side and looked down at her with the old, fond expression in his eyes. It sent the blood rioting madly through her veins. Then she held out her arms and gave a great cry.

'Bill, oh, Bill *darling!*'

He picked her up and hugged her close.

'Little Cherry . . . what does this mean? Where are we? What on earth has been happening? Cherry, where are we?' He talked wildly and incoherently. His mind was befogged. He had slipped back into the past and for that one supreme moment of her life, he recognised and loved Cherry again. She knew it could not last; that in a few more seconds everything would be revealed; her duplicity; her bigamous marriage. She knew that every face would be turned from her. So she clung madly to Bill — revelled in his obvious anxiety for her. Her chestnut curls were white with dust; her face streaked with dust, and tears trickled down her cheeks. She said:

'Bill, Bill *darling* . . . '

For an instant his lips touched her mouth. Then the spell was broken. Phillip's voice — cold as ice — broke it.

'Cherry — Bill! What the hell do you two think you're doing?'

Bill raised his head. He was as pale as death. He let Cherry go instantly. She stood trembling and waited for the storm to burst over her head. Bill stared in a bewildered way from her to Phillip. He put a hand to his forehead.

'I — Mr. Bellairs — oh, God, am I mad, or dreaming,' he muttered.

'Where am I? What is this all about? Cherry . . . '

Now his gaze travelled to Jan Barnes. Cherry too looked at her. The young nurse was pale too, and she was dabbing at a cut on one cheek with her handkerchief. Her dark eyes were frightened. For she had seen that mad embrace between Bill and Cherry and had realised that his memory had returned. Then her professional instinct asserted itself. She ran to Bill's side and took his hand.

'You're all right,' she said. 'Keep quite calm. Don't try and think too much. Keep quiet, please, Bill.'

He gave her a dazed look, then said: 'Hullo, Jan.'

Cherry began to stammer something but Jan turned on her. 'Don't say another word for the moment please — for his sake. This has got to be handled carefully.'

Phillip stood there dabbing at a cut on his chin. He was ashen. He was staring as though mesmerised at the overturned monster car. Two cars raced down the dusty road, the chromium sparkling in the sunshine. They were going at such a rate they did not even notice the accident. But the next one — a small Renault — pulled up.

The driver, wearing a beret, spoke excitedly in French. Cherry did not understand what he said, but Phillip answered and then the Frenchman nodded vigorously and drove on.

'He's fetching a breakdown,' said Phillip briefly, 'I told him none of us were hurt. For God's sake let's get off this road and sit under that tree.' He nodded to the green shade of an apple orchard. All four of them moved across, Bill leaning on Jan's strong young arm.

Phillip moved away and fumbled for a cigarette. Jan coolly lit one herself, and handed it to Bill who mechanically put it between his lips. He looked ghastly. His mind was incredibly confused but growing clearer with every moment. Jan said:

'Are you all right, Bill?'

'Fine,' he said laconically. 'Fine — only this — ' and he pointed to a torn trouser leg and bleeding shin. 'Superficial scratch. Wonder we weren't all killed. Lucky to be alive.'

Jan made him sit down with his back against a tree. A goat bleated nearby. The warm sun trickled through the leaves. Here was peace and all the hot beauty of the South. But in the hearts of the two men and the two women there was chaos. And in Cherry's heart a wild fear because now at last she knew that her hour of reckoning had come.

She darted forward and knelt down beside Bill.

'Look at me — darling — you do know me, don't you?'

He drew a long deep breath.

'Yes,' he said slowly. 'Of course, Cherry.'

'And me?' put in Jan, and her calm seemed as though it was going to desert her.

'Darling Jan, of course.' He broke off

and gave a smothered cry, his gaze returning to Cherry. The tangle of bright curls, the wonderful beauty of those long hazel heavy-lidded eyes, the slim seductiveness of that graceful figure — all was familiar to him then. Back went his memory — flashing back to the moment of their marriage in an English town. Hoarsely he said: 'Good God! Cherry — you and I are married, aren't we?'

Phillip swung round and came up to them.

'What was that?' he asked in a loud voice, 'What was that you said?'

Cherry's heart gave a frightful jerk as he uttered those words. The storm had broken. She quailed under it. In that terrible hour she would gladly have died. Jan turned from Bill and put her face in her hands. Phillip, who had been watching and listening, closed his eyes until they were glittering slits. Cherry could neither move nor speak. She was stricken dumb. Bill spoke again.

'Cherry and I are married. Yes, I'm

remembering it all now. That Saturday morning, we were married by the Local Registrar. We were starting off on our honeymoon when that lorry knocked me down. I suppose I lost my memory. It is a long time since then. Jan — what have I done?' He broke off. He looked back at Cherry. 'Cherry, this is too awful,' he gasped and his face was white and his eyes sick.

Phillip moved forward.

'This wants some more explaining,' he said in that cold voice of his. 'Cherry happens to be *my wife*.'

'I — but no,' said Bill hoarsely. 'It's impossible. She was married to me.'

'When,' rapped out Phillip.

'On the morning before my accident . . . ' Bill's brain had grown clearer, he spoke more decisively.

'Then I'm sorry. I beg to inform you that she wasn't free to marry you.' said Phillip ironically. 'She married me in London a few weeks before your heroic rescue of the child.'

There was dead silence. Bill swung

round on Cherry. He stared. She put a hand up to her throat. She felt finished; helpless! Like any criminal caught at last. And these were her judges; these three people . . . Phillip, Bill, Janet . . . all of whom stared at her with their amazed and accusing eyes.

'Cherry,' said Bill in a rough voice. 'What have you to say? Speak up — come on girl, for God's sake. Are we all mad or is it true? Have you done this frightful thing . . . it's *bigamy*. Are you really Phillip Bellairs' wife?'

'Yes,' Cherry said the word in a low sullen voice. 'I am. I married you, too, in Tunbridge Wells. I had no legal right to. I confess to it.'

'Then you are — *not* my wife,' said Bill slowly.

'No. I'm Phillip's . . . ' she suddenly burst into a torrent of weeping. 'I confess it. Oh, don't all look at me like that. You're not such angels. I've done wrong, yes, I know it. I wanted you both. I married you both and now you know it.'

'You — my Cherry — I adored you — trusted you,' said Bill slowly.

'I don't know that I ever trusted her,' came Phillip's caustic voice. 'But I didn't think she'd go so far as committing bigamy.' He cast her a venomous look. 'Damned little hypocrite,' he added. 'Going through a form of marriage with Bill Carew that Saturday. And you told me you were going home to mother. The lies you've told! The deceit! How many more crimes have you committed? What else have you done?'

Cherry shuddered and hid her face in her hands.

'Nothing,' she said in a muffled voice. 'Nothing at all.'

'But, Cherry — do you mean you were married to Mr. Bellairs all the time you were going out with me?' came Bill's shocked, amazing voice. 'When you were in that flat belonging to Mrs. Gerard — in her service.'

'Nonsense,' cut in Phillip. 'It was Cherry's own flat and mine and *she* was

Mrs. Gerard. We used that name when we were first married because I didn't want my family to know.'

'How perfectly ghastly,' Bill said. 'I can't believe it yet. Cherry — to have done such a frightful thing!'

Cherry raised her stricken face, drenched with tears. She flung out both hands to Bill.

'I loved you,' she said. 'It was because I couldn't live without you that I did it. Bill, forgive me, please!'

He stepped back. A look of such scorn, such indignation in his accusing eyes.

'You *loved* me?' he said. 'You call that love? I call it by another name.'

'Bill!' Cherry screamed. 'Bill, don't desert me. Don't judge me too harshly.'

He stared at the other two with embarrassment.

Phillip stepped forward and took her arm.

'Be quiet, Cherry,' he said. 'Let's end this. It's neither the time nor the place and Bill has had enough. You've done enough harm without making a scene like this in the middle of the road. Let us keep our heads for heaven's sake. The car's in the ditch and smashed up. The ruddy Cadillac has gone on — they didn't even stop to see what happened to us. We'll stop the next car that comes and ask it to take us back to Villefranche. We're only a few miles out, fortunately.'

Cherry began to struggle under Phillip's grip. She was in the throes of wild hysteria. Her nerves had gone to pieces — all control gone. She screamed and moaned for Bill.

'Bill — don't turn from me,' she gasped. 'I did truly love you, Bill!'

Then Janet Brown came to her aid. Her eyes were compassionate rather than contemptuous. She put an arm about Cherry's shoulders.

'Ssh! Take it easy, Mrs. Bellairs,' she said.

That hated name added fuel to the fire. Cherry hit out at the young nurse. She broke away from her restraining hand and rushed to Bill's side.

'Bill, don't turn on me, forgive me . . . Bill, don't look at me like that!' she shouted — like a madwoman.

He sat down on the grass verge and hid his face in his hands.

'My head is hurting — I can't stick it,' he muttered. 'For God's sake stop screaming.'

Cherry felt Phillip and Janet grip her arms. Then the world seemed to spin round her. Everything went black. She fell down in the dust.

17

Cherry was at home in her own luxurious bedroom, lying on her bed. She was undressed and the little French maid, Gabrielle, was bathing her mistresses head with eau-de-Cologne. Cherry recovered quickly. Full consciousness had brought its load of agony, of fear, of remorse. She sat up, her teeth beginning to chatter as though she was cold. Yet the sun poured through the slats of the Venetian blinds.

'Bill . . . ' she began.

'Madame, lie still,' whispered the little maid.

Cherry looked up at her wildly.

'What has happened? Where are the others?'

'Safely here, at home. *Mon Dieu*, but I thank God. You had a miraculous escape,' said Gabrielle fervently, as she dabbed Cherry's hot, wet forehead.

'The Monsieur, your husband, is all right. Monsieur Carew, he has the very severe headache, but Mam'selle Barnes she is quite all right. They have sent a — what you call breakdown — for the remains of the car.'

Cherry pushed the pretty, amiable girl away.

'I must get up at once,' she said hoarsely. 'Any dress — some shoes — quickly, Gabrielle.'

'But will not Madame rest? She fainted in the road and was unconscious all the way home in the car that picked up *tout le monde*,' began the maid.

'My dress — at once,' Cherry demanded.

With a head that was on fire and every limb shaking, Cherry dressed. She powdered her deathly face and Gabrielle brushed her distorted curls. Then she fled out of the bedroom downstairs. She wanted to see Bill and to hear him tell her that he had forgiven her before he went out of her life forever. She ran through the sunlit hall of the beautiful villa into her grand salon. Her heart gave a great bound of relief as she saw Bill alone. He was sitting in an arm-chair, his head between his hands; a half-finished brandy-and-soda beside him. Cherry was glad that neither her husband nor Janet were there. She ran forward and spoke his name.

'Bill!'

His stern, pale face looked at her. He sprang to his feet. He tried to walk straight past Cherry, but she caught his arm and clung to it frenziedly.

'Bill, don't go — don't refuse to speak to me. I can't stand it!' she said with a great sob.

He paused. He turned to her. In his eyes she read pain, pity, contempt. She laid her face against his sleeve.

'Bill, forgive me. I did love you. Honestly — whatever else I did — I loved you.'

'Please do get up,' he said. His voice was as cold as ice.

Cherry looked up at him tragically.

'Won't you try to remember when I was Cherry Brown — your own Cherry — and be a little sorry for me.'

'I don't want to remember the past at all,' he replied, and tried to draw his hand from her feverish fingers. 'It's all too frightful. It appals me.'

'You did love me, too,' Cherry said.

'I suppose I did,' he admitted. 'But I wish to God I had never got my memory back. I would be much happier. It drives me mad to think that I ever believed in you and of the vile way you behaved. Not only to me, but to Phillip Bellairs. Damn it, hadn't you any scruples?'

'I'm sorry — I'm dreadfully sorry now,' she whispered. 'I suppose I was mad. I married Phillip because his money tempted me, but as soon as I'd done it I realised I loved you. I always did love you, Bill. Try and believe that.'

'I don't want to. Please let go of my hand and go away and leave me alone.'

'No,' Cherry pleaded. 'Bill, you must

say you forgive me.'

'I can't,' he said with an effort. 'It was too utterly vile . . . what you did is beyond forgiveness. You're guilty of bigamy. That morning at Tunbridge Wells you behaved like a criminal — you deceived me and Bellairs. Then you ask me to believe in your *love*.'

'I may be crazy but I did love you,' Cherry insisted wildly. 'I did — oh, I did. Bill, I shall throw myself into the sea — I shall kill myself if you won't just say you forgive.'

He bit his lip. Cherry could see that he was not his normal, kindly self. She had hurt him beyond pardon. He said, hoarsely:

'If it's any use to you to hear me say the words, okay, Cherry, I forgive you. I'll try and regard you as a lunatic. That's what you are. One can forgive a lunatic. But I do beg you to leave me alone now and let me try to forget it all.'

Cherry looked up at him, her eyes filled with tears. He could see that the girl was, indeed, suffering. Her agony of grief, of contrition, was genuine. She said:

'Thank you — thank you for forgiving me. What can I do to make up for it, Bill?'

'Nothing,' he said coldly. Cherry let his hand go and he moved away from her, his hands in his pockets, his head bowed.

'There is absolutely nothing you can do. Our — farce of a marriage — is automatically dissolved. It was — not legal.'

Cherry hid her face in her hands, as she stood in that beautiful Italian salon which no longer had any meaning, any beauty for her. Her marriage to Bill would automatically be wiped out. She was less than nothing to Bill — the one being she had adored, and for whom she had committed the sin of bigamy. Suddenly Cherry could not resist a last, jealous word, stung from her by the sharpest pain.

'I'm all alone now. At least *you* have

— someone else. You have *her*.'

He looked at her quickly, his eyes softening.

'Yes, I have Jan. And when things are cleared up I hope to marry her.'

Cherry shuddered with jealousy.

Bill added: 'Good-bye, Cherry. I am going back to England to-day. I doubt if we'll meet again.'

He turned and walked out of the salon.

Cherry looked after his retreating figure. An agony so intense that it was almost insupportable, overwhelmed her.

'Bill, Bill,' she called, her voice thick with grief.

The drawing-room door closed quietly after him. He had gone, wishing only to forget Cherry. She had betrayed his love and he had left — never to return.

She never saw Bill again. It was the end of her mad, wild love-affair. She was face to face with the consequences of her own mad conduct.

There was to be no peace for Cherry for many a long, dreary month after her parting with Bill Carew. She wondered what all her beauty and charm and the gifts God had given her had brought her but disaster? She realised that she had misused her gifts — and lost everything. And the greatest of all the losses was that of the man she had loved. She knew she would never be able to forget Bill Carew.

After that last bitter scene with Bill, Cherry shut herself in her bedroom, refused to see anyone. Jan came to the door and asked if she might speak to Cherry. But Cherry felt too bitterly envious of her to want to make friends with her, or endure her pity.

'No, go away,' Cherry said, when Janet wanted to see her.

'I'm sorry about everything. I'm going back to England with Bill,' she called back to Cherry. 'Good-bye, Mrs. Bellairs and God be with you.'

Cherry maintained a spiteful silence. And Jan went away.

Cherry watched these two leave the villa. From her window she watched them, heart-sick and desolate. She took a last close look at Bill. Only to see him tenderly help Jan into the car. She saw him take Jan's hand and hold it; saw him give her one of his old, sunny smiles to which she responded. Then the car moved away. Cherry cried out under her breath.

'Good-bye, my darling.'

Bill had gone. Cherry knew that he would forget the bitter past and find true happiness with Jan.

That night Phillip came to Cherry's room. He found her already in bed. She was so worn out with crying, she lay motionless with a dim shaded light — unable to raise her aching head.

When Phillip came in, she felt sick and ashamed all over again as she read the complete contempt in his eyes. He was very bitter; very cynical; very brief in what he had to say. And there were no words of pardon from him, but Cherry wanted nothing. She had never loved him and now, when everything was over, she was completely indifferent to him.

He said:

'I'm not going to waste words telling you what I think of you. You're too wicked for words. You damn nearly ruined Carew's life and you've tried to make a mess of mine.'

'Well?' Cherry said, sullenly. 'What are you going to do?'

'Get rid of you in the quickest way possible,' he said brutally. 'I haven't the slightest wish to live with you under the same roof an hour longer.'

Cherry shivered and turned from his gaze.

'That goes for me, too.'

'Then at last we agree. The difficulty is how to get rid of you.'

'Divorce me — I don't care,' Cherry broke out wildly. 'I don't care about anything any more.'

'I don't think I want a divorce just now,' he said. 'In spite of the damnable way you've ignored the fact, I have a decent name and reputation to live up to. It upset my family and friends when I married you, and now I'm not going to have my name blazoned through the Press again and upset them all again.'

'Well, I don't suppose you'll allow *me* to divorce *you*.'

'Under no circumstances. So we'll have to fall back on the three years desertion business.'

Lashed by the utter coldness and callousness of his voice, Cherry said:

'And supposing I refuse to desert you?'

'I don't think you will,' he said, his eyes narrowing. 'For I wouldn't hesitate to make your life a hell if you did. I would also refuse to give you a single pound-note ever again. You still like money, don't you, Cherry? It's all you ever did really like. Well, I'll allow you enough to live on if you do exactly what I tell you.'

She flung herself face downward on her pillow. She felt so sick at heart and fundamentally so ashamed of herself she did not really care. But a leopard cannot change his spots in an instant and that overwhelming love of what money could buy still stirred, coiling like a little serpent in her heart. She said in a muffled voice: 'I agree. Tell me what you want me to do.'

'I thought you'd come to your senses, but my dear Cherry what I'd like to do if it hadn't meant such publicity, is to put you where you belong — behind prison bars. *Bigamy! Charming!* And not only have you wrecked my life but Bill Carew's. One of the most decent fellows I've ever met!'

Cherry beat her clenched fist on the pillow.

'I know — I know — don't keep telling me things like that — I know it all, and I wish I'd married Bill in the first place and been poor with him instead of rich with you.'

'I consider he was damned lucky to escape. I hope he'll be very happy with that nice nurse. I've '*had*' glamour girls. In your case what lies under the glamour is too ugly.'

Cherry sat up, teeth clenched, eyes blazing.

'Who are you to talk like a priggish judge?'

'You pipe down, my dear, or you won't get four-pence out of me.'

The mental and physical sickness returned to Cherry. She wished she were big enough to tell him to go to hell and take his money with him, instead of which she muttered:

'Oh, all right. But I *am* sorry, believe it or not.'

'I couldn't care less — just oblige me by packing your things and clearing out of this villa. I'll ring the airport and get you a seat on the next plane.'

'But you — '

'What I do isn't your business any longer. I shall return the villa to the Marquis, of course, and go back to London. You know my solicitors. If you want me, you can deal with me through them in future. All I can say is roll on the three years and the sooner I am quit of you, the better. If you don't behave yourself, I'll know about it, and that'll be the end of your allowance.'

She felt cornered and the lowest thing on earth. All the time she had a torturing memory of the scornful look she had last seen in Bill's blue eyes — and the thought that he and Jan were happily in love and that she would soon be forgotten by them utterly.

'I shall get rid of the Grosvenor Square flat,' Phillip was saying. 'Where you go and what you do on your allowance is your affair but I advise you to watch your step. The next time you break the law you won't find yourself let off so lightly — even your good looks won't save you.'

'Oh, leave me alone!' said Cherry, goaded beyond endurance.

'Good-bye,' he said and turned from her toward the door.

She made no attempt to call him back. If love was dead in Phillip's heart, it was equally dead in hers. She was merely surprised and somewhat relieved to think that he meant to give her enough money to live on. But a horribly blank future stretched in front of Cherry Bellairs, nee Brown.

Automatically she rang for Gabrielle for the last time and told her to pack everything.

The maid looked at her out of the corners of her eyes and said: '*Oui, Madame.*'

Cherry turned her face to the pillow again. Now the scalding tears came soaking into the linen, and this time they were genuine tears not only of self-pity but of remorse. A decent impulse that had come too late in Cherry's life. She felt a sudden distaste for the magnificent villa and her whole idle, wasted life. She felt even that it might be good to go back to Dalescombe and stay at the little cottage with her mother. When her sisters learned that she was separated from Phillip, they would ask questions. Even if she could not tell them the truth they would suspect that she had made a failure of things. And Phillip, in his hatred, would not hesitate to let the whole district know that he wanted to get rid of her. Only one person in the world would hold out her hand — and that would be her mother, whom she had always neglected.

What a little beast I've been, thought Cherry, 'Oh, Bill, Bill!'

★   ★   ★

There comes a moment in the life of every man when he is faced with the cross roads — one sign leading to the good and the other to the bad. For the second time Cherry Brown reached those cross roads, and it was then at last that she turned in the right direction.

It may be that in losing Bill Carew — and because of the black days and nights following the exposure of her crime — she acquired a new and better philosophy. Things went deeper. She was made aware of the transience of the 'fitful fever' called life, learned that love

— real love — must walk hand in hand with self-sacrifice.

She never saw Phillip Bellairs again. Bill Carew and Jan passed out of her life. She knew from their mutual friends that the two were married. She saw in time that handsome, well-remembered face smile at her from all the papers. *Carew* the new British boxing champion. In the house of a friend she even saw him appear on a television set — interviewed by a sports commentator. It made her feel so sick to see him and brought back the past so vividly that she had to go quickly out of the room, but on the whole she accepted what had happened, and began to work out her own salvation as best she could.

At first she was received as she had anticipated with loving tenderness by Mrs. Brown. But the old woman died shortly after Cherry's return to the village and Polly married. The cottage was sold up. Cherry went away. Not to glamour. Nor even to the old life; but to a very different one. With an almost agonising desire to be at peace with her conscience and to regain her self-respect, she took a job in a Home for Blind Children. She worked hard — often on her hands and knees. There was no varnish on her finger nails now. No lazy, luxurious life, for as 'Miss Brown' she worked among the afflicted children and became their idol. From them alone she felt she received genuine love, and as time passed her old mad longing for pleasure and money came to a complete end.

There was one more short and bitter hour for Cherry — when she saw the announcement in the paper of the birth of a son to the well-known boxer, Bill Carew; and a photograph of Jan, with her baby in her arms.

Cherry saw it while she was having her tea with the rest of the staff in the Blind Children's Home. She looked for a moment at Bill's child, and thought: '*It might have been mine. The happiness that Jan knows might have been mine, too.*'

She looked out of the window. It was a Spring day. A crowd of the blind children were playing one of their grave games holding hands. She heard them shouting, and dried her eyes. She put down the paper and a certain peace stole over her.

This was her mission in life. This was the way she was working out her redemption. She walked out into the garden and joined the children.